What the critics are saying...

"Jagged Gift has spellbinding suspense, hot sex...A very intense, gripping novel." ~ *Ecataromance Reviews*

"Dark and very emotionally driven...A masterpiece of romantic suspense and the paranormal." ~ *Enchanted in Romance Reviews*

"JAGGED GIFT by Nikki Soarde will have you quickly turning the pages with great anticipation until the very last word is read." ~ *Romance Junkies Reviews*

Nikki Soarde

JAGGED GIFT

ELLORA'S CAVE
ROMANTICA PUBLISHING

An Ellora's Cave Romantica Publication

www.ellorascave.com

Jagged Gift

ISBN #1419953885
ALL RIGHTS RESERVED.
Jagged Gift Copyright© 2005 Nikki Soarde
Edited by Sue-Ellen Gower
Cover art by Syneca

Electronic book Publication August 2005
Trade paperback Publication April 2006

Warning:

The following material contains graphic sexual content meant for mature readers. *Jagged Gift* has been rated E-rotic by a minimum of three independent reviewers.

Ellora's Cave Publishing offers three levels of Romantica™ reading entertainment: S (S-ensuous), E (E-rotic), and X (X-treme).

S-*ensuous* love scenes are explicit and leave nothing to the imagination.

E-*rotic* love scenes are explicit, leave nothing to the imagination, and are high in volume per the overall word count. In addition, some E-rated titles might contain fantasy material that some readers find objectionable, such as bondage, submission, same sex encounters, forced seductions, and so forth. E-rated titles are the most graphic titles we carry; it is common, for instance, for an author to use words such as "fucking", "cock", "pussy", and such within their work of literature.

X-*treme* titles differ from E-rated titles only in plot premise and storyline execution. Unlike E-rated titles, stories designated with the letter X tend to contain controversial subject matter not for the faint of heart.

About the Author

৯১

Nikki lives in a small town in Ontario, Canada. In the midst of the chaos that comes with raising three small boys, working part-time as a lab tech in a hospital blood bank, and caring for her ever-adoring husband, she dreams up her stories. Nikki's work is an eclectic combination of romance, mystery, suspense and humor with characters that have plenty of room to grow.

Nikki welcomes mail from readers. You can write to her c/o Ellora's Cave Publishing at 1056 Home Avenue, Akron OH, 44310-3502.

Also by Nikki Soarde

৯১

And Lady Makes Three (*anthology*)
Balance of Power
Duplicity
Ellora's Cavemen: Legendary Tails III (*anthology*)
Phobia

JAGGED GIFT

౬౨

Trademarks Acknowledgement

~

The author acknowledges the trademarked status and trademark owners of the following wordmarks mentioned in this work of fiction:

Heineken: Heineken Brouwerijen B.V.

Glenfiddich: William Grant & Sons Limited

Mustang: Ford Motor Company

Ferrari: Ferrari S.p.A.

Datsun: Nissan Jidosha Kabushiki Kaisha

Steinway: Steinway, Inc Corporation

Limoges: Bernardaud Porcelaines de Limoges

Prologue

ॐ

"How do you feel?"

Marty heard the voice. It came to him as if from the far end of a long, dark tunnel. He struggled to open his eyes, but the lids felt like they'd been stitched together.

"How do you like it?" asked the voice.

"Like what?" he asked, his lips functioning just a little better than his eyes.

"Like being a victim." Pain zinged through his jaw as a set of knuckles cracked against the side of his face. His eyes flew open and he looked up into the eyes of his tormentor. They were pale gray—gray like a chip of slate, and just as hard. They peered out from behind a shank of blond-streaked hair. The face was deeply tanned and peppered with freckles. A beach bum. He'd been abducted by a fucking beach bum.

"That's better," said the beach bum, backing away. "I was getting tired of waiting." Funny, though, he didn't *sound* like a beach bum. The tone of his voice was dark somehow, with an edge like serrated steel that grated across Marty's nerves.

"Waiting?" asked Marty, his vision swimming. His head still felt thick but it was coming back to him now.

He remembered screams, blood, a soft throat beneath his fingers, a rush of adrenaline, a noise behind him, a flash of pain in his shoulder, and then...nothing. "Waiting for what?"

"Waiting for you to wake up." The beach bum pulled something out of his pocket and placed it to his lips. He struck a match and lit the joint, inhaling deeply. He blew out a thin stream of smoke. "So we can finish this."

Marty's confusion was mounting. As well as his fear. It wasn't just due to being drugged and dragged to some dark, dank basement in the middle of God-knows-where. At least he assumed it was a basement. The lack of windows and the dampness gave him that impression, but it was just that—an impression. As was his sense of foreboding, of latent terror.

"What are you talking about?" asked Marty, his voice high and shaky. "Finish what? Why did you bring me here?"

The beach bum took another drag. "Why, to teach you a lesson, Marty." And then Marty noticed the gun stuffed into the waistband of his black jeans. "And, I'm happy to say, it'll be the last lesson you'll ever have to learn."

Chapter One

ഇ

Race rolled over and reached across the mattress to draw Lisa close. His arm met an empty pillow.

He opened his eyes to find watery sunshine streaming in through the slats of the blinds and noted that the digital clock read only 6:27. He frowned, listened for water running in the bathroom but heard nothing.

"Lisa?" When she didn't answer he rolled out of bed and reached for his robe. Worry had already knotted in his gut, and knowing it was completely irrational did nothing to ease his fears. He trudged out of the bedroom, through his living room and followed the aroma of coffee to the kitchen. He found her there, dressed in a long slim skirt and cotton tunic, sitting in the breakfast nook sipping coffee. A suitcase sat at her feet.

He stopped in the doorway and stared, waiting for her to acknowledge his presence. She didn't. She just kept staring out the window at the breathtaking Vancouver skyline and the ocean that glittered in the distance. She sipped from her mug.

"Lisa?" he tried again. "What's going on? Do you have to go to Tokyo again?" He hated when she had to go out of the country.

At last she turned to look at him, her curtain of black hair swishing across those delicate cheeks. She was so small and fragile, so helpless. Although she'd scream at him for saying so, physically it was the god's honest truth. If he wanted to he could pick her up and snap her in two like a dry twig. Any man could.

And that terrified him.

"No, I'm not going to Tokyo," she said, setting her mug onto the glass tabletop with a soft click. "I'm going home."

He blinked, bewildered. "Home? As in to visit your folks?"

"No. Home, as in I'm moving back in with Tessa until I can find my own place." She wrapped her hands around the mug and drew it closer, as if establishing a barrier between them. "Moving in here was a mistake. I knew it from the beginning, but I tried to deny it. I kept hoping…" She shook her head, turned her gaze away.

"Kept hoping what?" He crossed to the table and grabbed a chair. He pulled it out but didn't sit down, instead he wrapped his hands around the curved backrest and held on for dear life.

She lifted her gaze to his. "I hoped that once I moved in you'd feel more settled, more…comfortable. I thought that if I was here you'd feel more secure about me, that you'd give me a little more breathing room. That you'd stop holding me so tight and not have to monitor my every move."

"Are you saying I'm possessive?" he shot back. "Controlling? You think I've got abusive tendencies?"

"What? No. God, no. That's not what I'm saying at all."

"That's sure what it sounds like."

She set her eyes on him, her gaze hard at first, but gradually her expression softened. She pushed away from the table and stood. She stepped over to him and grasped his hands. "It's not about control, Race. I know that."

"And it's not that I don't trust you. It's just—"

She pressed her fingers to his lips. "It's that you're worried for my safety. I always suspected that, and your suggestion that I carry a gun on my business trips confirmed it." She shook her head. "I know it *sounds* sweet, but it's not…natural."

"It's not natural to worry about my girlfriend who's traveling alone through a foreign country?"

"Not to the level that you take it, no. And you know it's not just when I'm out of the country. It's *all the time*, Race, and some time ago I began to feel it like some sort of…burden. Like I was responsible for the anguish that you felt every time we were apart." She let go of his hands and stepped away. "And I can't take that kind of responsibility. Not anymore."

He did understand on some level, but hesitated to admit it. He didn't want to acknowledge that he was, in some way, responsible for driving her away.

"You don't love me," he argued.

"You know I do."

"Well then, you don't love me enough." It came out harsher than he'd intended.

She picked up her suitcase, her expression sad. "Maybe I don't." She strode toward the door, her steps so quick and purposeful it took him a moment to realize what was happening and he had to sprint to catch her.

He reached the door a moment before her, and braced his hand against it.

She glared at him. "Are you going to keep me here against my will? Is that it?"

He dropped his hand to his side. "You think I'm capable of that?"

She said nothing, and somehow he knew that if he pressed her, the answer would be "yes". And maybe she did believe it, but that didn't make it true. He was capable of a lot of things, but not that.

There were tears in her eyes when she pulled the door open.

"So, that's it?" he asked bitterly. "That's all you have to say?"

Her hand still on the knob, she said softly, "There's more to it than the worrying, and the way you suffocate me."

"More? Isn't that enough?"

"We've talked about this before, but you refuse to deal with it. You refuse to acknowledge that it's even an issue."

He clamped his jaw shut.

"See? Just last night I told you how much it bothered me, but you wouldn't even discuss it. Wouldn't even consider my suggestion."

He stuffed his hands into the pockets of his robe. "I don't get it. As I recall you had no less than two orgasms last night. How can you have a problem with that? How can it be an *issue*?"

"It's about more than an *orgasm* count, for God's sake." He took a step back in the face of her anger.

She took a deep breath and blew it out. "It's about more than sex, Race. It's about intimacy and sharing."

"I share a lot with you."

"And there's so much more that you hold inside. I always get the feeling that there are things you're not telling me. Important things. Dark things." Her voice had dropped to a barely audible whisper.

He didn't bother to deny it, and in the knife-edge silence that followed she studied him. After several tense moments her mouth opened as if she was about to say something more, but apparently she changed her mind. She clamped her mouth shut and adjusted the shoulder strap of her bag.

"You need help, Race. A psychologist, or a therapist, I don't know. Maybe even one of those sex therapists. I've heard there's a good one in town."

He opened his mouth to laugh, but no sound came out.

"I just know that you need help and I can't be the one to give it to you." She stepped into the hall. "I'll send for the rest of my things in a few days." And without so much as a goodbye she walked off down the hall and out of his life.

He closed the door softly behind her and leaned against it. He raked a hand through his mop of short, blond hair and considered.

"A psychiatrist?" he said aloud. He laughed then, but the chuckles clogged in his throat. "A *sex* therapist?" He stalked off toward the kitchen and allowed the rage to overshadow the pain of being left alone. He was used to it after all, used to being abandoned by the women he cared about. He was used to being alone and he was good at it. It was what he did best.

He glanced at the key ring that hung by the door, the one with the rabbit's foot fob. It looked so innocent hanging there, all furry and sweet, but of course that was a sham. There was nothing innocent about it. He thought of the door that key unlocked and the secrets hidden inside, and smiled a grim smile.

Being alone wasn't his only talent. There was one thing he did better.

* * * * *

"Are you coming to the party?"

Race added a column to his spreadsheet and began to enter the appropriate debits and credits.

"Did you hear me?" asked Eric Devlin, Race's foremost client, oldest friend. And biggest pest.

"I heard you."

"Then answer me." Eric's grin was easygoing, mischievous. Rakish. It was the kind of smile only a rich man who is young and handsome and confident with his place in the world can smile. The goatee and long, dark hair pulled back in a neat ponytail accented the effect. More than one woman had swooned over that smile, but so far none of them had managed to hold onto him for longer than a few months. Or was it the other way around?

"And make sure it's the right answer," persisted Eric.

"I don't do parties."

"Beh!" exclaimed Eric, his voice a convincing rendition of a game-show buzzer. "Wrong answer." He grabbed the back of the supple leather office chair and spun Race to face him. "You do parties. As I recall you did more parties in college than I did. Toga parties were your specialty."

"Toga parties are for kids. I'm not a kid."

Eric rolled his eyes and slumped back against a wide set of French doors. The doors, intricately inlaid with a rainbow of stained glass, led out to an expansive pool and patio area. Eric had money and liked to spend it. He didn't believe in scrimping, and he considered his home, including his study, to be a showpiece.

"Need I remind you," said Eric, reaching for a glass of lemonade he'd set on a nearby trolley, "that this is my *birthday* party we're talking about here? And it will have about as much in common with a toga party as a Ferrari has with a Datsun?"

"You'll never let me forget that I owned a Datsun, will you?"

"Never. Come."

"No."

"It's my birthday."

"I'm busy."

"No. You're sulking."

Exasperated, Race pushed the chair backward and erupted from his seat. He stalked to the bar on the far side of the room and proceeded to pour himself a glass of Glenfiddich. "Lisa left three days ago. Is it a crime to need a few days to regroup?"

"The party isn't until Saturday. That's five days from now, and it's exactly what you need. You need a distraction, something to get your mind *off* her."

Race sipped from his whiskey and gazed at his friend over the rim of the glass. "Are you sure you're not setting me up?"

"Setting you up?"

"Yeah, you know. Inviting a bevy of beautiful babes in the hopes I'll get nabbed by one? Maybe get laid?"

Eric laughed, shook his head, and sat down in the chair Race had just vacated. He leaned forward, braced his elbows on the desk and gazed at Race as the smile slowly slipped from his face. "What went wrong, Race? I thought you two were good together. I liked her. I thought she would last."

Race took a sip of whiskey and savored the heat as it tore its way down his throat. "So did I."

"Then what? What happened? Why did she leave?"

Maybe it was the whiskey, maybe it was the intensity of Eric's gaze. Or maybe it was just that Race had been carrying this around for so long that it had begun to feel like a lead weight around his neck, like a hunk of concrete that was dragging him down to the depths of some very deep, very dark, very *cold* ocean. Maybe sharing a bit of it would lighten the load.

"She said I held her too tight, that I didn't give her enough breathing space."

Eric nodded slowly, as if he understood.

"You agree with her?"

Eric tilted his head, his gaze distant as if searching for the most diplomatic answer. "You are a little protective, Race. A little intense." Eric sipped from his lemonade and said thoughtfully, "You're kind of like a big bonfire. Even twenty feet away a guy can feel the heat on his face, and it makes him want to step back. Couple that with the way you hold a woman so close…"

Race gritted his teeth and studied his whiskey. No one understood how fragile, how *vulnerable* they all were. No one really grasped the full scope of the dangers that threatened women, knew the monsters that lurked in the shadows. He knew monsters, knew them intimately. He'd seen them, he'd touched them. He'd dipped his hands into their blood.

He just hoped he hadn't become one of them.

"Is that all?" asked Eric, when the moment and Race's nerves had stretched to the breaking point. "Did she say anything else?"

Race, still feeling a little raw from the breakup as well as from his friend's implied judgment, gripped the glass so tightly he was surprised it didn't shatter. He glared at Eric. "Do you really want to know?"

"Yes. If I know then maybe I can help."

Race slugged back the last of the whiskey and slammed the glass down on the bar. "I'm lousy in bed. How's that for a confession? Do you get your jollies out of that? Huh? Do you?"

Eric's eyes went wide, and then, to Race's amazement he laughed. He laughed long and hard. "Oh, that's rich," he said, when he'd managed to draw breath and had wiped the tears of glee from his eyes. "That's the best laugh I've had all week."

Race said nothing.

"Come on, buddy. Out with it. What's the real reason?"

"That *is* the real reason. She had…issues with how I make love."

His jaw set, and his eyes appraising, Eric remained silent for a time. "Okay, I think I get it. It's not that you're not a *good* lover, is it? It can't be, because I've been compared to you often enough that I'm lucky it didn't give me a complex."

It was true that in their college days Race and Eric had occasionally…shared or swapped women, and many of them hadn't hesitated to tell the other man tales of how his buddy performed — or didn't perform — in bed.

Eric continued. "I've talked to enough women that you've been with to know that you give out orgasms like other men give out chocolates."

Despite the dour mood Race couldn't keep his lips from twitching.

"It's something…else, right? Something more complex than that."

Race strode over to the desk and glowered at his friend. "Can I get back to work? I do have other clients, you know."

Eric grinned. "Maybe, but none of them pay as well as I do." He stood and stepped away from the desk, allowing Race to sit down. "And you're evading the question."

Race bent over the keyboard. "It's none of your business."

"Come to the party and I'll promise never to mention it again."

Race groaned his frustration. "You won't stop hounding me until I agree to it, will you?"

"Nope. And if you come I promise you won't be sorry. I've got something special in mind."

Race looked at his friend, narrowed his eyes. "No blind dates."

Eric shook his head, but his eyes glittered with something that Race couldn't quite identify. "No blind dates." He raised his right hand. "Scout's honor."

Chapter Two

୫୬

Candra stepped out of the limousine, stood on the flagstone walkway. Her short cotton skirt billowed around her thighs and the wind whipped her long, chestnut hair into a froth. She brushed the strands off her face—and gaped.

"It's something, isn't it?" asked Megan who had slid out of the limo behind her.

Candra blew out a slow breath. "Eric said he was having a *house* party. He didn't say anything about a…a…castle."

Walls composed of enormous granite blocks stretched to the sky. Well, she conceded, maybe not to the sky, but at least three stories, if not four. Turrets and chimneys rose from the roofline like knights poised for battle, and the windows— Candra blinked, and then blinked again. The windows, all glowing with flickering candlelight and set deeply in the two-foot-thick walls, were made up of dozens of tiny panes of glass set in leaded frames and inset with stained glass in a rainbow of jewel-toned colors. She had this surreal feeling that she'd stepped back in time to seventeenth-century France, complete with baroque cathedrals, decadent kings and peasants pounding at the gates.

Megan laughed and linked her petite, china-doll arm with Candra's.

At five-foot eight-inches, despite a figure that many had referred to as "willowy", Candra invariably felt like a bumbling giant beside her five-foot-nothing friend.

"You've been inside his offices," said Megan, pushing a few strands of midnight-black hair behind her ear. "You know how flamboyant he is, and how successful the company has been."

"I suppose. I mean I know computer software is a real cash cow for Bill Gates and all, but still…" She turned a suspicious eye on Megan. "How much does he pay you, anyway? Suddenly I'm having second thoughts about picking up lunch tabs all the time."

Her blue eyes sparkling, Megan led her past a splashing fountain and lush rosebushes toward the front door—the hand-carved, solid oak front door. "He pays well enough, but I'm still just a secretary, you know. I won't threaten your ego by trying to pay for your dinner."

They climbed the stone staircase. "Ego?" asked Candra with an innocent bat of her eyelashes. "I don't have an ego."

A short guffaw burst from Megan's throat as she pulled on the enormous silk tassel that hung from the archway above the door. "Candra, an elephant could crawl inside your ego and hibernate." She smiled sweetly.

"Elephants don't hibernate."

"Whatever."

A bell chimed somewhere in the bowels of the house, and a moment later the door opened. "Megan!"

Candra found herself enclosed in a one-armed bear hug. Megan struggled for breath in the other half of Eric's fierce embrace. He smelled vaguely of wine, but not offensively so, and the fact that his shirt was already pleasantly rumpled confirmed that Eric had been enjoying the festivities to the fullest.

He released them and smiled, turning his gaze from Megan to Candra and back again. His eyes sparkled despite his liberal consumption of alcohol. "I'm so glad you came. It just wasn't any fun without you."

Megan arched a finely tweezed brow. "Eric, you could have fun with a ball of string and a button."

He draped his arms around both their shoulders and steered them inside. "Now Megan, I thought we agreed that little hobby would be our little secret."

Chatting and teasing, they moved through the foyer. They strolled beneath a soaring ceiling, across mirror-like marble floors that reflected the light of a thousand tapered candles, and past a sweeping staircase that looked as if it had been lifted directly out of the pages of *Gone with the Wind*. Except for the occasional guest who seemed to be wandering aimlessly, exploring the magnificence around them, the foyer was empty. As they approached the far side of the room, however, the pounding of a heavy rock beat and the murmur of a hundred conversations heralded their approach to the main knot of guests.

Candra and Megan each nabbed a glass of wine from a passing waiter and stepped through an archway into the thick of the party.

The room teemed with life. There had to be a hundred guests, if not more, lounging on leather couches and leaning against the solid oak bar, laughing and talking and dancing. The room was enormous, but would likely still have been crowded if not for the fact that the patio doors had been flung wide and guests had spilled out into the moonlit night.

"Your house is amazing," breathed Candra, lifting her gaze to her host. "I want to thank you for inviting me."

Eric released both women, glanced at the crowd and then turned back to them. "Thanks, but…" He grimaced. "You might not thank me after meeting Race. He's likely to eat us both alive when he finds out what I've been up to."

"I wouldn't worry about that. I'm a lot tougher to choke down than a shrimp canapé." She turned her attention to the milling throng. Both Megan and Eric had described Race to her, but she doubted she could recognize him amidst the sea of strange faces. "Speaking of which, where is he?"

When Eric didn't reply she turned her attention back to him.

He considered her for a moment. "Are you sure you want to do this? I've been thinking about it, and I'm afraid I've put you in a rather…awkward position."

Before Candra could answer, Megan rested a hand lightly on her boss's arm. "Why don't I let you two talk? I'll be out dangling my feet in the pool if anyone needs me."

Eric growled. "Damn you, woman. You know how I feel about your ankles."

She winked at him over her shoulder. "Be a very good boy, and maybe I'll let you see my knees." She sauntered off, hips swinging.

He watched her go and Candra watched him. And wondered…

"Eric?" she prompted, when Megan had disappeared into the crowd.

He shook his head briefly and turned back to face her. "Right. So, you're sure?"

Candra had never been one to back away from a challenge. "I'm sure."

"Okay then. Follow me. The bugger has slipped off somewhere, but I've got a pretty good idea where to find him."

He led her through the thick of the crowd, wending his way around furniture, smiling and calling greetings to friends as he eased past them and urged them to try the hors d'oeuvres and drink more champagne. They reached the far side of the room and stepped out onto the expansive patio.

She stopped and gave herself a moment to take it all in.

The elaborate patio was in reality more of a courtyard. The space, framed on three sides by the U-shaped mansion, afforded every wing of the house access to the pool and the view that came with it. The house sat on a rise, so the fourth side of the patio square opened out onto a magnificent view of the Pacific Ocean. The night was clear and the moon at three-quarters. It hung low over the ocean, its silvery light scattered and reflected in the waves that darted across the water's surface.

Lilies and candles floated in the enormous kidney-shaped pool, and bouquets of roses and carnations adorned the dozen or so tables that dotted the pool deck. There had to be at least as many guests out here as there were inside, and it took Candra a moment to spot Megan sitting on the edge of the pool chatting with a man that Candra didn't recognize.

Eric paused in his tracks and followed her gaze. He frowned, but his hesitation was brief. He grasped Candra by the hand and continued to lead her on. "This way."

She scanned the edges of the crowd as they walked but saw no one that even remotely fit the description Megan had given her.

At last they reached the far side of the courtyard and stopped before yet another set of French doors inlaid with stained glass. "Just as I thought." A mischievous smile played across his lips and he leaned in close to the doors. "Listen."

She frowned, but then at his direction leaned closer and perked up her ears. She heard the soft lilt of piano music, and after a few moments identified the piece. "That's the 'Moonlight Sonata'," she said, incredulous. "Is that—"

"It sure is." With that Eric pushed open the doors and burst into the room. "Race, old man," he bellowed, shattering the delicate mood of the music, "it's time you pulled your head out of the sand and joined the human race. Or at the very least joined my party."

Race's back was to them, his hands poised over the keys, his back rigid. "If your guests are representative of the human race, then I'd just as soon take my chances in the sand. It's tough to say which is more dry, the Sahara, or the conversation out on that patio." He still hadn't turned around.

Eric clutched at his chest. "Ooh. Cut to the quick. For a number-cruncher, Race sure has a way with words."

"And piano keys," added Candra. "What I heard was inspiring. I'd love to hear the rest."

At her voice, Race whirled around on the piano bench and leapt from his seat. "What the hell?"

"May I introduce Candra Brandt," offered Eric. "She's a friend of Megan's and I thought she was someone you should meet."

As Eric spoke, Race locked a pair of pale gray eyes on her and gradually the air between them began to sizzle. His eyes were magnetic, holding her gaze captive. She made no effort to break eye contact, but in her peripheral vision she got several very quick impressions. Tall, athletic and tanned, with freckles and blond-streaked hair. As Eric had said, he looked like the kind of guy you expected to see lounging on the beach in Malibu, but no one who had looked into those eyes could carry that impression for long. There was an intensity about him, an…energy, that was at once compelling and unnerving. She felt as if, with his gaze alone, he was stripping away her defenses, layer by layer, searching her soul, scratching away at secrets even she had forgotten existed.

For several irrational moments she waged a silent war, the instinct to turn and run battling the inexplicable urge to draw closer.

Abruptly, he shifted his gaze to Eric, and his hold on her evaporated. She blinked, and blew out a breath she hadn't realized she'd been holding.

"What the hell is this, Eric? No setups and no blind dates. You promised."

Eric shook his head and slid Candra a weary look. "Race is a social Neanderthal. He thinks 'tact' is a four-letter word."

"It *is* a four-letter word," growled Race, stalking toward them, "and so is exit."

He was heading for the door when Eric's hand darted out and grabbed his arm. "Race." In a heartbeat, Eric's tone shifted from light and teasing to low and earnest. It stopped Race in his tracks. "Hold on a minute and let me explain."

Race shrugged off his friend's touch, but made no move to leave. "What's there to explain? I told you I'm not interested in—"

"This isn't a setup. At least not in the way that you're thinking."

Race glared at Eric. "Well?"

Eric moved to speak, but Candra interrupted him with a hand on his arm. "Eric was concerned about you, and he thought maybe I could help."

"Concerned about me?" Race glared at Eric and the temperature in the room dropped five degrees. "And what, exactly, does that mean?"

Eric rolled his eyes and turned on Race. "Oh, for God's sake, Race, let's stop dancing around this. You've got a problem with intimacy and it's keeping you from finding happiness." He threw up his hands. "What the hell am I saying? It's making you downright miserable, and the only way it's going to get better is if you face up to it and do something about it. And as your best friend I can't stand by and watch you self-destruct. Not anymore."

"What did you *tell* her?" asked Race, his voice vibrating with rage.

Feeling the need to make her presence known, Candra stepped between the two men. "I'm a certified psychologist and I specialize in problems with intimacy and sexual dysfunction."

He turned that icy glare on her. "A *sex* therapist? Is that what you're trying to say?"

She drew back her shoulders and met his frosty gaze with what she hoped was enough heat to melt the polar icecaps. "No. Any Joe Blow on the street can hang up a shingle and call himself a sex therapist. I've got a doctorate in psychology and extensive counseling and sexual surrogate experience. I specialize in sexuality because it's an area that troubles a large chunk of the population, and because I'm good at helping people."

He stepped up very close to her—close enough that she could feel the heat of his breath and smell the spiciness of his cologne. "Well, I don't know what Eric told you, but I don't *need* your help. I'm fine."

"Well then, if you're fine you've got nothing to hide, do you?" She crossed her arms, but the barrier it provided felt completely inadequate. "Talk to me and prove Eric wrong. I have little doubt there's nothing you'd rather do than humiliate your best friend."

He blinked, apparently taken aback by this little twist, and Eric's laughter echoed through the room.

"She's got you there, buddy." Eric slapped Race on the back. "What do you say? Are you up to the challenge?"

"This is ridiculous," snarled Race, "I don't have to listen to this bullshit. I should just go home and open up that six-pack of Heineken I've been saving." But he didn't leave. He held his ground.

"I'll have a couple of bottles brought in if you like," said Eric. "Imported beer, a few minutes alone with a beautiful woman, and a chance to see me eat my words. How can you turn that down?"

Race lifted his gaze to hers again, considering. "Forget the Heinekens," he said slowly. "Make it a bottle of Glenfiddich, and you're on."

Candra smiled, relieved. "Good. I don't think you'll be disappointed."

Race ignored her. Instead, he continued to Eric, "And have it delivered to the guest room on the third floor. This is kinda personal, and I think I'd like a little privacy."

More than a little surprised, Candra arched her eyebrows and looked to Eric for direction. They had planned to approach Race in a crowd, and introduce her to him in a very casual manner. They'd hoped she could coax him into conversation, and that the presence of a crowd would ease the pressure on him. A one-on-one conversation alone in a room away from the crowd reeked of intimacy — the very thing Eric had said Race had a problem with. So far, though, Race had shot the plan all to hell.

Eric shrugged. "I guess I haven't got a problem with that. If you don't."

She turned back to Race, but his expression was benign, giving away nothing. So why did it make her so uneasy?

She made her decision. "All right. I have no objections." But even as she said it, she couldn't help wondering if she should have come up with a few.

* * * * *

Candra stepped into the room and shook her head in wonder. A hexagonal bed, constructed of polished mahogany, complete with not four, but *six* thick posts, served as the centerpiece for the room. A stone fireplace, bearskin rug, solid oak bookshelves, bar and elaborate entertainment center completed the ensemble. A pair of glass doors opened onto a large balcony. Laughter and the sound of someone splashing in the pool, drifted up from the courtyard below.

She shifted her gaze to Race who lounged against the bar, glass of whiskey already in hand. "Eric certainly has elaborate tastes."

"He's a fucking show-off. He does things just to get attention, and just because he can." He lifted the glass to his lips and drained it.

"That's a nice thing to say about your best friend."

He glared at her over the rim. "It's the truth. Case in point—you."

She strode to the bar and picked up the glass he had poured for her. "You think he brought me here just to show off? You don't think he did it because he cares about you?"

"Rich people think they can control everything. That they can *fix* everything. But you can't. Some things just can't be fixed."

She sipped and allowed the liquid to scorch its way down her throat. "So, you're admitting it. You're admitting that you're...broken. That you do have a problem that needs fixing."

He slammed the glass onto the bar. "I didn't say that."

"I think you did."

Suddenly he stepped very close to her, his body pressing her back against the bar, his arms bracketing her in like a pair of wrought iron bars. She could feel the pounding of his heart, feel the sturdiness of his chest and see the way his muscles corded in his arms and neck. She lifted her chin and risked meeting his gaze. As expected, it stole her breath.

"What are you doing?"

And then he did the unthinkable—he lowered his head and kissed her. He sealed his lips to hers, his mouth hard and demanding. He forced his tongue past her lips and she tasted whiskey and heat. She lifted her hands to his chest with the intention of pushing him away, but found her fingers fisting in the material instead. She gripped him hard, knowing she should let go, but unable to force her fingers to relent.

He wrapped his arms around her and pulled her against him, she felt his burgeoning erection, the hardness and fullness of it pressing against her cleft and filling her with a need she neither expected nor wanted.

His tongue thrust deeper, his embrace tightened and she felt completely overwhelmed. Lost. Grasping at a last shred of rationality, she tried to turn her head and break the kiss, but he wouldn't have it. He sank his fingers into her hair and held her firm, plundering her mouth and grinding his cock against her until she felt the dampness seep down her thighs.

And then he was gone.

She sagged against the bar, her legs suddenly too weak to hold her, and watched in wonder as he walked to the bed and sat down. He leaned back on his elbows and glared at her.

"Wh-what the hell was that?" She had wanted to scream it, but it came out as little more than a pathetic whisper.

"Was that the kiss of a man who is afraid of intimacy?"

She opened her mouth to retort and then, very slowly closed it again. As the blood gradually seeped back into her brain her thoughts cleared, and she considered the question. She stood up a little straighter. "Maybe."

His eyes went wide, and then narrowed. "All right. Get over here, and let's finish it."

She gaped at him. "Look, Race. I don't know what you think a therapist *does*, but let me assure you, this does not fall into the job description."

"Bullshit."

"Bullshit?"

"Bullshit. Did you think I wasn't listening when you listed your credentials earlier?"

A bit of heat crept into her cheeks. "You're referring to the sexual surrogacy I mentioned."

"I sure am, and I know full well what that means. You do a helluva lot more than just *talk* to your clients, and I figure what better way to convince you that I'm not in need of your services than to *show* you."

She took a chance and stepped closer to him. "Okay," she conceded, "I'll admit that as a surrogate I occasionally help my clients work through their problems with more...direct methods. *But—*" she raised a finger to drive home her point, "—that is always, *always* a last resort, after all traditional therapy methods have been tried and proved ineffective. Even considering that, I have often endured criticism from my colleagues for mixing what they consider two vastly different schools of thought on the subject. And I have no intention of jeopardizing my professional reputation further with this...this...*farce*!"

He looked at her then, pinned her with those steel-gray eyes of his, holding her captive as surely as a cat that has just pounced on a fallen bird. She couldn't move, could barely breathe. She silently wondered at herself and cursed her own inexplicable weakness.

His gaze never wavering, he slid off the bed and stepped over to her. He brushed a finger down her cheek, the touch so light it sent shivers skittering down her spine. "Are you saying you don't want me?"

She swallowed, and lied. "Yes. That's what I'm saying. And even if I did, it would be irrelevant. Now can we please sit down and—"

And then he was kissing her again. He crushed her mouth beneath his own, and pulled her body against him. Her heart leapt into motion and she had to struggle to maintain her hold on rational thought. She didn't want this. Correction—*couldn't* want it. Couldn't allow herself to want it.

But as his hands fisted in her hair and his tongue plundered her mouth, as his scent filled her nostrils and the hardness of his body pressed more firmly against her, need overcame rationality. Almost.

She shifted her hips a little—just enough—drew back her leg and with carefully calculated force slammed her knee into his groin.

She missed.

He must have sensed what was coming because at the last moment he broke the kiss and stepped away. He now glared at her, his gaze no longer cold, but hot as the center of a star. "Do you routinely try to castrate your clients?"

She allowed the heat to flare in her own eyes. "Do you routinely rape your friend's guests?"

The fire in his eyes flickered. She'd hit a nerve.

The muscles in his jaw flexed. "I wasn't going to rape you."

"Well, I don't recall consenting. What would you call it?"

Fists clenched and shoulders bunched, he stalked past her and stepped over to the balcony. He didn't step outside, just stood on the threshold gazing out over the ocean. Over the sound of the laughter and gaiety downstairs, she heard him say, "Well, then you may as well go. We're done here."

She stared at him, letting his words sink in. When his meaning had sifted through the emotional turmoil of a few moments before she narrowed her eyes, stalked over to him, grabbed his arm and yanked him around to face her. "So, that's it? You're just going to ignore this problem? Hope it just goes away on its own?"

"I'm fine."

"You're *not* fine. Eric tells me that you desperately want to find someone and settle down, but that six months is the longest you've ever managed to hang on to someone. He says you've lost some really special ladies, and that there is never an obvious reason as to why. He said that you never talk about your parents or your childhood, and the merest mention of that topic can send you off into a deep funk. He said you're *often* moody, and that he occasionally can't get hold of you for days on end, and then when you finally do resurface you can't seem to come up with any feasible reason for your absence. And then he told me that you admitted that the women you're with have some sort of specific complaint about how you relate to them during lovemaking. He said you didn't elaborate, but that the fact that you even mentioned it was cause for him to take steps and contact me." She rammed a finger into his chest. "So don't tell me that there's nothing wrong, because I know differently."

"I've lived with it for more than twenty years, *Doc*. I've managed just fine without you."

He didn't seem to realize that he'd just admitted to having a problem. She decided against pointing that out to him. "I don't think you're doing fine at all. And twenty years is far too long to live with something like this festering inside you."

His jaw clenched and he seemed to be considering it.

She continued, "You need someone to talk to, Race. Someone who's outside and can see things a bit more clearly, someone who won't judge you and who—"

"You really want to help me?"

She pressed her lips together and nodded. She meant it, perhaps more than she'd ever meant it before. For some reason she could see his pain—*feel* it—more clearly than she'd ever experienced with any other client. It was like looking at a beautiful painting that had been violated with a can of bright red spray paint. His torment was that clear to her, and the need to ease it overwhelming.

"Yes," she said. "I do."

"Then you can help me by leaving me alone."

His answer surprised her, but something inside her told her she needed to fight for him. If he wasn't going to do it then someone had to. And that someone was going to be her. "No."

He took a deep breath and tried to slice through her with his eyes. "What will it take to get rid of you?"

"I'll leave you alone when I believe that you've resolved whatever issues you have with intimacy. I'll leave when *I* believe you're fine."

He stepped very close to her again and she tamped down the urge to step back. "Well, I'm *telling* you you're wasting your time. I don't need you."

She chose not to point out that he had effectively just contradicted himself. This kind of vacillating was common. "I think you do."

"What will it take to prove to you that I don't?"

She licked her lips that had gradually gone very dry. "Well, once we've talked and explored your situation, once we've—"

"Talk is cheap, Doc. Action is where it's at." He combed his fingers through her hair. "Let's face it. Fucking me is the only way to know for sure."

He was baiting her, and she knew it. But at some deeper level, she also acknowledged that he was right. She hesitated to go this route, but something told her that Race was different, that he needed her in ways too complex and too profound to articulate. And she needed to help him in a way that even she didn't understand. She would do whatever it took to accomplish that.

She stepped closer, close enough that his chest brushed against her breasts. "All right."

His hand paused, a few strands of her hair still clinging to his fingers. "What?"

"You heard me. Give me your best shot, Race Kendall. Prove to me that you don't need me and I'll walk out that door and never come back."

He licked his lips, and for the first time she saw a hint of nervousness. "You're consenting?"

"Yes, Race. I'm consenting."

Chapter Three

৪৩

Race stared at her, uncertain of what he was hearing, hesitant to believe it, and even more hesitant to act. It had been a bluff—a bluff that he'd been certain she wouldn't call him on. But when she touched his hand, trailed a neatly filed fingernail up his arm, and curled those full, bronze-tinted lips into a smile that was at once coquettish and challenging—he accepted the truth. And he took action.

He plowed his fingers through her lush mane of chestnut hair and held her head firm as he ravaged her mouth with yet another of his famous kisses. Women had crawled over one another in pursuit of his kisses. His kisses were legendary and he knew it, cultivated the image that went with it. It was the stuff that came later that he couldn't seem to get right.

Her mouth was soft and deep, and inviting. He sank his tongue into her, sampling and exploring until her chest struggled for breath.

Damn, she was easy to kiss. Candra's beauty had struck him the moment he laid eyes on her. Tall and graceful, with long legs, hair the color of rich mahogany and eyes as warm and blue as a Caribbean sea. The first time he met her gaze he felt like he was sinking into a deep, warm ocean, and he'd been fighting to stay afloat ever since. He'd immersed himself in women before, and been left floundering. A couple of times he'd almost drowned, and he didn't intend to let it happen again.

It helped that Candra's interest in him was purely clinical. Once he proved himself to her, he never had to lay eyes on her again. That should make this easier.

He hoped like hell that would make this easier.

She wilted against him, giving herself over to the kiss and to him, and he felt a fresh desire stir to life. He dragged a hand down her back, across the whisper of material she called a blouse, and down to cup her ass. He jerked her against him, tight. He ground his cock against her cleft and she let out a soft groan of pleasure. Regretfully, he dropped his other hand from its silky nest in her hair, and grabbed her ass with both hands. It was small and fit his palms well.

His mouth still sealed to hers, he steered her backward, away from the balcony doors and any prying eyes, and back into the room. He kept going until she bumped up against the back of the leather couch that faced the fireplace. Stalled there for a moment, he bunched up her skirt and palmed the bare skin beneath. For a moment he thought she hadn't bothered with underwear, but then he found the tiny wedge of material at the top of her cleft. A thong.

He smiled and broke the kiss. She leaned against the couch back and sucked in a deep breath. She looked up at him, her eyes smoky with desire. "What about the bed?" she whispered. "It's such a beautiful—"

He had moved his hand around to the front and slipped it beneath the material. He cruised over her clit and sank his finger into her without prelude. He found her open and wet and added another finger to increase the pressure. He began to pump her and her eyes glazed, her fingers dug into his shirt, and then her head fell back onto her shoulders.

He nudged her legs further apart to allow himself deeper access and began massaging her clit with his palm. Her chest heaved and sweat glazed her skin. He bent his head and drew his tongue across her throat, tasting her sweat and drinking in her scent.

Abruptly he drove his fingers still deeper and at the same moment, sank his teeth into her throat. She cried out and arched her back, driving her hips forward and pulling her shoulders back. As if she was fighting with herself, not sure whether she wanted to stay or run away. He wrapped his free arm around the small of her back and held her firm as the orgasm shook her to her core.

As the last of the spasms shuddered through her, Candra's eyes fluttered open. She found Race looking down at her, his gaze as intense and compelling as ever, and yet distant. Despite the physical contact they had just shared she felt no closer to him than when they first met.

She opened her mouth to articulate it when, abruptly, he bent down and scooped her off the floor. "Race?" she squealed in surprise. "What are you doing?"

But no explanation was necessary when, a moment later, he knelt down and laid her on the white bearskin rug before the fireplace. The fur was plush and warm and she luxuriated in it as Race quickly whisked off her skirt and thong, and cast them aside.

"So, you're not finished?" she asked, all innocence. "I did kind of wonder."

He said nothing.

He stood and she watched in appreciation as he whipped off his T-shirt and exposed the chest and shoulders that had only been hinted at before. Broad and lean, with well-developed muscles that seemed to favor definition over bulk. For a moment she thought he was hairless, but then realized that the blond hairs on his chest were virtually invisible against his tan. The tan, however, highlighted the assortment of scars that dotted his torso, their pale color standing out in stark contrast to the bronze of his skin. She wondered about them, but not for long.

Her attention was drawn to the rippling muscles of his belly—and the button that he had just popped open. He undid the fly and pushed his jeans and briefs down over his hips. Her breath caught at the erection that jutted out before him, and she drew herself up to her knees and reached out to touch it.

She hadn't intended to participate in the lovemaking, had intended to act as more of an observer. This was his opportunity to prove himself to her, and she had no wish to interfere with his style or technique. However, even she had her limits.

She drew a finger down the length of his cock, traced his balls and then drew a line back to the tip. She wrapped her hand around him then and moved forward, intending to taste him, but was stopped by his hand on her shoulders.

She watched as he slowly sank to his knees before her. He grasped her hands and placed them on his chest. She frowned up at him, uncertain as to what he wanted.

"Touch me," he said then, his voice a low, thick whisper.

She smiled and complied, running her fingers lightly over his chest and shoulders, down the sinewy length of his arms and across his knuckles. She explored his belly, tracing the hollows between the ridges and pausing briefly at one particular intriguing scar beneath his rib cage. It was shaped like a crescent moon, and appeared quite deep. She moved on quickly though, not wanting him to think she was focusing on an imperfection. She vowed, however, to ask him about it. Later.

His skin had grown damp at her touch and she noticed that, impossibly, his erection seemed to have grown. She skimmed her fingers over it only briefly, however, before reaching around to grip the firm rounds of his ass. They tightened at her touch and she sank her fingers deeply into taut muscle.

She looked up at him, felt the electricity sizzle, and felt the dampness grow again between her own thighs. "Aren't you going to touch me?" she asked.

He nodded, grasped her wrists and inched away from her. He nodded toward the rug, but once again she had no idea what he wanted. "Lay down," he ordered softly. "On your tummy."

At once puzzled and intrigued, she did as he asked, lowering herself to the soft, plush fur of the rug. It tickled her pussy and she wanted to feel it everywhere. "My blouse," she said, raising herself. "I want it off."

She reached for the buttons and soon had them all undone. She removed the blouse and cast it aside, secretly surprised that he had made no move to help her. Nude now, except for the lacy bit of lingerie that was her bra, she was pleased to feel his hand press against her belly. His palm was warm and firm as he explored her ribs and tummy and reached lower toward her pussy. His fingers parted the lips of her sex and massaged her clit, dipping into her wetness and spreading it over her with a touch that sent little bolts of electricity zinging through her. She closed her eyes and allowed herself to ride on his touch, but the attention was brief. He withdrew his hand and she opened her eyes to see him bring his fingers to her lips. He arched his eyebrows suggestively and smiled for what she realized was the first time.

She took her cue and drew his fingers deeply into her mouth. Tasting herself and the muskiness of his own flavor as she wrapped her tongue around his fingers and sucked them clean.

He made a low growling noise in his throat and reluctantly withdrew his fingers from her mouth.

The muscles in his jaw flexed, and she suspected he was exercising some secret stash of self-control as he motioned for her to lay down once again on the bearskin.

She took a deep breath, made an effort to calm the frantic beating of her heart, and complied. As she lowered herself to the rug she heard the snap of a latch and saw with interest that he had opened a small cupboard beside the fireplace. He pulled out a plastic bottle, and when he popped it open she smelled the vague essence of cinnamon.

She lay on the thick cushion of fur and, now unable to see what he was doing, she wondered. He didn't make her wait long.

She heard him pop the cap closed and when his hands touched her feet they slid over her skin easily, leaving behind a slick coating of massage oil.

"A foot massage?" she whispered, the smile creeping through her. "If you're trying to impress me—" His thumb sank into her arch and she groaned. "—it's working."

She said nothing after that. Couldn't have spoken if she'd wanted to. His touch was expert, as if he had some sort of divine knowledge of every one of her muscles and knew exactly which ones to probe for greatest effect. He rubbed his thumbs down the length of her arch, and with firm circles massaged the tops of her feet. She didn't even know she *had* muscles there, but he found them and made them sing with pleasure. As a final touch he lifted her feet from the rug and suckled lightly on each of her toes. She would have giggled except that she was far too drunk with his touch to expend the energy.

And then he moved to her calves. He drew his thumbs down their length in long, slow strokes that eventually graduated to small, hard circles. He found knots and coaxed them into submission with the diligent persistence of a child begging a parent for just one more cookie—softly, sweetly, relentlessly.

His fingers worked down her shin, again finding muscles she barely knew existed and eliciting pleasures she'd never dreamed. Not even her knees were immune as he continued his magic and worked his way up to her thighs. He paused only once to replenish his supply of oil before he bent back to his task.

The white fur rug might have been a cloud, for as much as she felt like she was floating toward heaven. But then his hands reached her ass and a new pleasure shimmered through her. Her eyes drifted open at the provocative way his fingers cruised over her curves, his thumbs dipping suggestively toward her pussy.

She parted her thighs and lifted her hips, urging him to do more, but he ignored her, proceeding at his own torturous pace. He massaged her buttocks and the small of her back thoroughly, his thumbs and fingers only skimming over her pussy enough to keep her wet and wanting.

Then, abruptly, her eyes flew open at the touch of his tongue. He laved her ass cheeks, drawing lazy circles and lapping up the flavorful oil. At last his thumbs sank into her pussy and she groaned and pushed her hips back toward him.

He drove his thumbs deeper and at last urged her to lift her hips from the rug. She drew her knees forward until she sat on her haunches. She lifted her hips and was rewarded with the sensation of his thumbs driving deep, her cheeks being parted and the touch of his tongue on her anus.

"Oh...God," she groaned as he circled the sensitive flesh and darted inside her. His thumbs pumping her all the while.

The sensations were overwhelming, but she realized she wanted something that he wasn't offering. "I...want...you." She knew it was cryptic, but hoped he would understand.

He must have, because a moment later his cock stabbed inside her, withdrew and drove in again, every thrust deep and fast and breathtaking. He was thick and hard, and it wasn't long before she felt her pleasure spiraling toward climax.

But then the thrusts eased off and she felt something else. She held her breath as he pressed an oil-slicked thumb against the opening of her anus. The touch was a question and she could only manage a soft moan of an answer. He massaged the muscle as he continued gentle movements of his cock. When, at last, his thumb pressed past the boundary, he abandoned all efforts at tenderness. His cock thrust hard and his thumb pushed deep.

He splayed his other hand across her belly to hold her firm as he increased the force and tempo of his assault.

She whimpered at the steady crescendo of sensations, feeling as if her body had been lit on fire and was dangling by a thread over a precipice. The thrusts continued, his belly slapping against her buttocks, his cock filling her and the pleasure building as he pushed his thumb even more deeply inside her.

When his other hand slipped low on her belly and pressed firmly on her clit, the world shattered.

The added pressure inside her ass seemed to strengthen the orgasm and magnify the sensations as the pleasure pounded through her and the breath whooshed out of her. Her orgasm persisted, the walls of her sex driving Race to his own climax.

He held her firmly against him, his body rigid as he pumped himself into her and a few moments later they both collapsed in a heap of sated, sweat-soaked human flesh.

Candra leaned back against the bar and swirled the ice in her whiskey as she watched Race pull on his shirt. She appreciated the way the cotton hugged his frame, but already found herself remembering how he looked without it. She shook off the images and took a sip from her glass. The fire that etched its way down her throat was a poor distraction.

Race smiled at her as he reached for his own glass and the expression transformed him from handsome to breathtaking.

"What are you grinning about?" She kept her voice even but it was an effort. Needing a moment to regroup, she dragged her gaze away and studied her tumbler. "It almost seems like you enjoyed yourself."

He laughed and the sound made her tummy lift.

"Yeah," he said, still chuckling, "it almost seems that way, doesn't it. And I dare say you had an okay time, too."

She shrugged. "Mmm. I guess it was okay." But she couldn't suppress her grin. "Okay, so you massage like a pro, and that was one of the strongest orgasms I've ever experienced. Does that make you happy? Are you going to be able to walk through doors without hitting your head on the doorframe?"

He took a sip of whiskey. "It's never been a problem before. But I always have a couple of humble pills in my pocket in case of emergencies."

"You hear that a lot, do you?"

"On occasion." His grin was irrepressible, and he was obviously pleased with himself.

"Mmm." She drained her glass and set it on the bar. She hated to burst his bubble but there was no point in postponing the inevitable. "So, how does this week look for you?"

His hand paused, the glass hovering in midair. "Pardon?"

"I'm just wondering when we could book you in for your first appointment."

The smile fell away, leaving behind an expression of utter astonishment. "A-appointment?" he stuttered. "What the hell are you talking about?"

"You know exactly what I'm talking about."

He glared at her.

"What happened over there—" she motioned to the bear rug, "—was an exercise, correct? It was your chance to show me whether or not you had issues with your sexuality, and I think we established the answer to that clearly enough."

He crossed his arms, his feeble attempt to protect himself from the words he didn't want to hear. "I don't hear you complaining, Doc. You came twice and you admitted that it was some of the best lovemaking you've ever experienced."

She shook her head. "I didn't say that. I said it was one of the best *orgasms* I've ever experienced. Lovemaking and intimacy is another issue entirely."

"I don't see the difference."

Very softly she replied, "And that's part of the problem."

"Oh, for Christ's sake." He threw up his hands. "I know the difference between sex and lovemaking, okay? But I'm not in *love* with you, am I? Surely you can't expect me to pretend otherwise. I *assumed* you could take that into account as part of your..." He waved his hand in the air as he searched for a word. "...evaluation."

"Of course I did, and I understand that."

"Then what the *hell* is the problem?"

Outside, the party noises had escalated. The music and laughter had grown louder, but even over the noise they clearly heard a woman scream and the splash that followed. The laughter and shouts confirmed that she'd been thrown in the pool and was none too happy about it.

"I'd really rather discuss this in my office," said Candra at last.

"No. Tell me now, or you can count me out."

"I don't think—"

Race's cry of pain cut through her words like a blade. She stood there and watched, dumbstruck, as his body jerked and fell. It was as if he'd been snagged by an invisible hook and yanked backward. He landed on the floor and lay there, his eyes wide and staring as his chest heaved, struggling for breath. Other than that he didn't move.

"Race?" she cried, dropping to her knees beside him. He'd gone deathly pale and when she touched his forearm she found it cool and clammy. "Race, what's wrong?"

Still no response. Battling panic, she touched a finger to his carotid and counted the beats. His pulse was rapid but regular, but his breathing concerned her. It was harsh, coming in ragged gasps as if his chest were constricted or the air was being forcibly sucked from his lungs.

A seizure? she wondered. Seizures could take many forms, she knew, from mild narcoleptic episodes where the subject fell asleep for barely perceptible spans of time, to the full-blown grand mal seizures that most people associated with the term.

She was just about to reach for a blanket to cover him when he blinked, moaned and turned his head toward her.

"Race?" She found his hand and squeezed. "Can you hear me now?"

He wrenched his hand from her grasp and turned away, rolling onto his stomach and drawing in his elbows as if struggling to right himself. He mumbled something but she couldn't make it out.

She leaned in close, deciding it best not to touch him. "What? What did you say?"

47

"Out." The word came out as a rasping whisper.

"Out?" What the hell did that mean? "What's *out*?"

He pulled in his knees and forced himself up onto all fours. "Get out." He turned his head and locked that piercing gaze on her. "Now."

Before she could assimilate that, he let out another sharp cry and fell onto his side. He didn't remain still this time, however. Instead he began to writhe as if battling some unseen demon. "Jesus," he groaned. "Holy Jesus."

She crawled closer, tears of terror brimming in her eyes. "Let me help you. I want to do something but...I don't *understand*." She'd never seen anything like this before, and didn't know what to do. She hated the sensation of helplessness.

"Get out. Leave me alone."

She shook her head. "No," she said, certain that he had descended into some sort of dementia and didn't know what he was saying. "I can't do that."

He'd struggled onto all fours again, and his breathing seemed to have settled somewhat. Sweat, however, had beaded on his face and now dripped from his nose. He lifted his head and locked his gaze on her again. "Eric," he breathed. "Go...get...Eric."

And then he closed his eyes and made a sound that she could only describe as a whimper.

"Eric." She nodded and sprang to her feet. "Yes. I'll go get Eric." Grateful for the mission and the sense of purpose it gave her, she backed away, heading for the door. He had crawled toward the bed and was pulling himself up toward the mattress.

Her hand found the doorknob. "Good. You lay down and I'll be back with Eric in two minutes."

He nodded, said nothing.

"Two minutes." She bolted out the door and fled down the stairs.

* * * * *

"Eric!" screamed Candra, pushing her way through yet another knot of guests. "Where's Eric?" She looked frantically from face to face but was met only with drunken shrugs or looks of sympathetic puzzlement.

"Eric!" She wound her way through the crowd, scanning faces and pleading for someone—anyone—to help her find the host of the evening.

Finally someone in the crowd shouted out, "He's in the pool." There was a hoot of laughter. "And he's drunk as a skunk."

"Great," she grumbled, heading for the patio doors. "Just what I need."

She burst out onto the patio, screaming Eric's name and ignoring the reproving looks that many guests tossed her way. She reached the edge of the pool and found him at last, floating on an inflatable chair, cuddled up with two blondes, laughing and guzzling champagne directly from the bottle. She noticed Megan sitting at a table on the far side of the pool, her back turned, her shoulders rigid.

Candra didn't have time to deal with that right now.

"Eric Devlin," she screamed, "get your ass out of the pool and up to the third floor."

At last he turned a bleary gaze her way. "What?"

"It's Race. There's something very wrong, and he needs you."

"Wrong?" He blinked, digesting this information. "What do you mean?"

"I don't have time to explain, and if you don't get your ass over here this minute I'm going to come in there and get you."

"Candra?" Megan had rounded the pool and now stood beside her. "What's going on? Can I help?"

"I don't know." She was relieved to see that Eric had abandoned the two beauties and had already crossed the distance to the side of the pool. She reached for Megan's hand and took strength from its familiar touch. "I just don't know."

Less than a minute later the three of them were racing up the final set of stairs that led to the penthouse bedroom.

"A seizure?" asked Eric, suddenly sobered by her news. He was taking the stairs two at a time. "What kind of seizure?"

"I don't know. I'm not even sure that's what it was. Don't *you* know?"

They reached the landing and followed Eric's mad dash down the hall. "No." He paused, his hand on the knob. "Why would I know?"

"Well…he asked specifically for you, so I figured…"

Eric frowned and shook his head. "This is all news to me." And then he pushed open the door and burst into the room. "As far as I know Race has never been sick a day in his life."

The three of them stepped inside and stood there, staring. Empty. Race was gone.

Candra blinked as if that would help clear her vision and make Race reappear. It didn't work.

"But he was here a minute ago." She rushed to the bed and motioned to the rumpled covers. "See? He was using the blankets to pull himself up. This is crazy. Where would he go?"

"The bathroom." Eric headed for the en suite bath and Candra felt like an idiot for not thinking of that. Maybe Race had felt nauseated or needed a drink of water.

But a moment later Eric appeared in the doorway, eyebrows pulled together in concern. "Nothing. He's gone."

Candra and Megan exchanged a glance.

Candra clenched her fists. "But that doesn't make sense. When I left him he could hardly stand, let alone *walk*."

Megan squeezed her hand. "We should search the house. Maybe he's not aware of what he's doing and he got lost." She turned to Eric. "Right? Why don't we organize a search?"

But Eric had walked to the bar and pulled out a phone that was apparently kept hidden back there. "Eric?" asked Megan. "What are you doing?"

"Just a minute." He dialed a number and held the receiver to his ear. He stood there, listening for what seemed like an eternity. At last he set down the receiver and breathed a heavy sigh. "He's gone."

"What?" Candra stepped forward. "What do you mean, *he's gone*?"

Eric shrugged. "Just that. He's disappeared and there's no point in looking for him. At least not for a couple of days."

Candra gaped at him, struggling to find a shred of logic in what he was saying.

Eric rounded the bar and rejoined them, wedging himself between them and draping an arm over each of their shoulders. He guided them toward the door.

"Look, you'll just have to trust me on this. In the fourteen years I've known him this has happened more than a dozen times."

"The seizure?" asked Candra. "I thought you said—"

"No. I've never witnessed something like that. I'm not sure what that's all about, but I do know that he always has his cell phone on him. Always. On the rare occasion that he turns it off, that means he wants to be left alone. Doesn't want you to look for him, and doesn't want to be found. You won't find him at his apartment, and you won't get hold of him any other way. In two or three days he'll surface again. He'll be fine and he'll act as if nothing's happened." They reached the landing at the top of the stairs. "In other words there's no point in asking where he's been or what he's been up to, because he won't tell you anything."

Candra pulled away from Eric's touch and clenched her fists, confused and fuming.

"By the way," asked Eric, "what happened up here? Did you talk him into coming to see you?"

Candra looked at him, struggling to sift through what had just happened and understand what he was asking of her. "Oh yeah," she said at last. "He's coming to see me, all right." She stomped off down the stairs. "I'll make sure of it."

* * * * *

Race lay beneath the hedgerow that lined the back of Eric's property. Sweat and dew soaked his skin and tears streaked his cheeks. His eyes remained closed and his breathing slowed as the last of the images flitted across his vision, the last tendrils of pain snaked through his body, and his *source*, as he had come to call the women through whom he experienced the pain, gave herself over to the inevitable.

This victim had fought hard, refusing to give her attacker the satisfaction of an easy conquest as he violated her body and attempted to dominate her spirit. Her effort had been valiant, but had only succeeded in prolonging her pain, and extending Race's own agony.

He'd felt each blow that she felt, experienced all the same terrors, endured all the same humiliations. He'd struggled for breath with her as her attacker gripped her throat and he'd screamed in pain as the knife pierced her belly.

As the episode waned and her heart slowed, he felt his connection to her begin to weaken. He felt the withdrawal of the blade as little more than a gentle tug and heard her killer's last words as if they had been shouted from across a vast canyon.

"Fuckin' bitch," echoed the vile voice. "Stupid fuckin' whore."

Her last ragged breaths seemed to flutter across his skin like the whisper of angel wings. And when it was over he was left only with a fleeting image of a child. The little girl she had left behind.

Then he corrected himself—*wasn't going* to leave behind.

Still too weak to sit up but strong enough to clench his hands into a pair of mutinous fists, his eyes flew open and he whispered to the stars, "She won't lose her mother. Not if I have anything to say about it."

What he'd seen was not carved in stone. This small glimpse of tomorrow night was subject to change. He'd learned that much. The future was a malleable thing, as nebulous and changing as mist over the water. And just as hard to control. But there were always options— opportunities—and he did his best to exploit them and shape the future into something a little more palatable. A little more...*just*.

Very slowly he sat up and brushed the last of her tears from his eyes. He checked his watch. The episode had been a long one, lasting a little over an hour. She was a fighter all right, and that was good news for him. It would make his job that much easier.

He took a few deep breaths, drawing in the scents of damp grass and sleeping lilies, and considered what he needed to do. From the little glimpses he'd had he now had to deduce who she was. He had to find her, find out where she would meet her killer and then he had to get there. And change everything.

There was so much—so many things to attend to, and so many questions that needed answering. But the enormity of the task neither intimidated nor discouraged him. He wouldn't let it.

He stood up and brushed the leaves and grass from his clothes before stumbling off into the night.

He had a little less than twenty-four hours and not a minute to waste.

Chapter Four

ဆာ

Candra reached for another slice of pizza, sat back in her chair—and marveled. Every visit to Eric's mansion revealed new wonders. The party the night before had taken place almost entirely in the west wing of the house, but after Race's disappearance she'd done a little wandering and thought she'd managed to see pretty much everything. But when she and Megan had arrived tonight, their arms piled high with pizza boxes, Eric had shown her yet one more wonder that she had apparently missed.

With her knees drawn up under her chin and her feet propped on the edge of the chair, she made an incongruous picture in Eric's gothic dining room. Set against a backdrop of intricate stonework, flickering torches and carved wooden chairs upholstered in plush red velvet, she would have been more at home ripping the leg off an enormous roast pheasant rather than plucking olives off a triple-cheese-and-pepperoni special. At least her feet weren't on the table, though. Eric had absolutely no sense of propriety at all.

She took a bite and chewed slowly. "So, what do you *think* he does during these little…sojourns?"

Eric leveled his gaze at her over his enormous pewter goblet. "I told you already. I don't have a clue."

"But you must—"

"Candra." Eric set his goblet down with enough force to slosh some red wine onto the table. "You're not listening. I've asked him about it numerous times, and I never get anything more eloquent than one of his famous cold stares, or maybe a few glib comments or insults."

"He's just a very private person," added Megan. Her voice was soft but the look she cast at Eric was somewhat reproving. There had been a subtle but undeniable tension between them all evening, and Candra wondered if it had something to do with the two blondes from the party. Megan and Eric had never even been on an official date and yet…

Eric snorted. "Private? That's the understatement of the year. The man keeps secrets better than a gay priest. I've known him more than ten years and I still know don't know much more about him than I do about the guy I hired last month to clean my office."

Candra nibbled away the last of the cheese and tossed her crust back into the box. She picked up her wine and cradled the goblet in her palm. "So he keeps a lot inside."

Eric nodded.

"That always makes therapy a challenge, but it's not exactly rare in my line of work."

"Well, I wish you luck."

"It might help if I could get a little…jump on things."

"Jump?"

"Tell me about him."

"I already told you about him."

She shook her head. "You told me about his problems with relationships. I want to know more. I want to know everything."

Eric scrutinized her, his gaze long and level as he considered her request. At last he picked up his wine and, very deliberately, crossed his ankles on the carved oak table. Intricate brass inlays reflected the torchlight and lent an aura of magic and whimsy to the room.

Eric took a leisurely sip of wine. "Like I said, I've known him more than ten years and I still don't know much."

"I'll take whatever I can get. Every little bit helps, you know."

He nodded. "Okay. Did you have anything specific in mind?"

"Well...what about his family? That's always a good place to start."

Eric and Megan exchanged a brief glance and to Candra's surprise it was Megan who answered. "He doesn't talk about his family."

Candra waited for Megan to fill the blanks that were so glaringly empty, but when Megan offered nothing further, Candra prodded her. "Sometimes what we *don't* say is more revealing than what we *do* say."

Megan stared at the half-eaten slice of pizza she held in her hand and then abruptly tossed it onto her plate. "It was after my mother died a few years ago. He didn't come to the funeral but it was just a couple of weeks after the services that Eric took him and me out to lunch. He made a point of extending his condolences and he was very sweet about it, but for some reason I couldn't let it go at that. I guess I was just in the mood to talk about it or something, so I asked him if his mother was still alive."

At that Megan and Eric shared an obviously uncomfortable glance.

"What?" asked Candra. "What happened?"

Eric was the one who answered. "He got real quiet and kind of cold...you know, like only Race can get?" He shook his head. "But then all he said was that his mother had died years ago, and two minutes later he made an excuse to leave."

Megan was twirling a napkin around her finger. "For some reason I felt *horrible* after that, as if I'd been really insensitive or stupid or...something."

Eric tapped the table. "That's ridiculous. You were trying to be considerate, for Chrissake. I had never told you that he'd been raised in foster homes, and it was a perfectly reasonable question. You had nothing to be sorry for."

Candra perked up. "Foster homes? You never mentioned that to me before."

"I didn't think of it. It's not something that we talk about frequently."

"Well, I'm glad you thought of it now."

Eric reached for the bottle of wine to refill his goblet, but when he gripped the bottle his hand froze. "Hold on a second."

"What?"

"I just remembered something. It's not much but it may be significant."

"Eric!"

Chuckling softly, he continued, "It happened back in college and that was so long ago…" He shook his head as if coming back to himself. "We were drunk one night after one of my famous toga parties and we got to talking about family. Now, you gotta understand, when I say drunk I mean *drunk*. Plastered. Wasted. We'd been loading up on brandy and had gotten about as drunk as two college boys can get, and that's saying something."

Candra caught herself smiling.

"So, it was in that state that he said something that, to this day, gives me the chills. He was talking about what he remembered about his mother, and what a wonderful person she was, and then, real casual-like, he mentioned how horrible it was to witness his own mother's death."

The wine in Candra's mouth turned sour. "He said what?"

"You heard me. At the time I was too drunk to pay much attention, but I did ask him about it later. At first he didn't want to tell me but when I pressed him he finally told me."

Eric dropped his feet from the table and shifted uncomfortably in the chair. "The thing is he swore me to secrecy. I promised to never tell another living soul."

Candra leaned forward. "I can appreciate that, Eric, but this could be so important. It could be the key to everything, and if I don't know what I'm dealing with..." She let the suggestion hang in the air, let the weight of responsibility settle on Eric's shoulders. "You brought me into this because you want to help him. You started it, Eric, you have to help me finish it."

Eric narrowed his eyes. "You fight dirty."

"Of course I do."

He sighed, took a sip of wine. "All right. He and his mother were in a horrible car accident. They were on a back road and a transport truck crossed the center line and hit them. The car rolled several times and his mother was..." He took another sip of wine. "She was impaled on the steering column, but didn't die immediately. He was hurt but conscious, but he said the car was so crumpled he couldn't move. He was trapped there beside her, watching her bleed out while they waited for help to arrive."

Candra took a deep breath. "He had to sit by, helpless, watching his mother die and feeling like he should do something."

"Yeah. Something like that."

She nodded, assimilating that.

"Wow," said Megan. "Small wonder he prefers not to talk about it. I can't imagine dealing with something like that." The enormous grandfather clock in the corner struck ten, the ponderous chimes echoing through the room and lending a foreboding air to the already somber atmosphere.

Megan added, "I don't blame him for trying to forget it."

Candra nodded, choosing not to voice her own thoughts. That sometimes the things we try the hardest to forget are the things that most need remembering. Suppressed memories were like an emotional minefield, and Candra had no intention of allowing Race to continue to struggle through that minefield. Or at the very least she didn't intend to let him do it alone.

*   *   *   *   *

Race's watch read 10:10—exactly five minutes before he'd felt the first blow the night before. Crouched in the shadows between buildings, he'd watched as a rusted-out Buick had pulled into the motel lot and parked. The driver, a tall, slender man in his late fifties with mouse-brown hair and unusually sharp features had gotten out and waited impatiently at the door to Room 15, while his companion had fussed with something in the passenger seat. After a few moments the door had opened and a woman in miniskirt and skin-tight T-shirt had gotten out and joined the man, allowing him to lead her into the room and close and lock the door behind them.

Race fingered the counterfeit key he'd had made earlier in the day after he'd checked into the room for a few hours and headed down to the local hardware store.

It had been easier than expected to track down the motel, since in his mind's eye he had a clear image of a pink flamingo beside a pair of numerals styled of interlocking bamboo. A quick scan of the yellow pages had revealed only two "Tropicana" motels in the greater Vancouver area, and of those, only one displayed the flamingo logo beside the door number. He also had the name Stephanie Lowen firmly lodged in his brain. The name of the victim.

It wasn't always that easy. His connection to this victim was unusually strong, but it didn't always work out that way. Sometimes what few images managed to filter through to him, were fuzzy or simply not helpful in his quest to track down the victim and the location of the incident. Twice he'd failed to make the necessary connections and had been unable to track down the information before the twenty-four-hour deadline had passed. Both times local newspapers had featured stories of brutally murdered women within the next couple of days.

He didn't intend to let that happen again. Not when it was within his power to stop it.

With the motel room door firmly closed and the deadline approaching, Race pulled his pistol from its holster, slipped out of the shadows and stole over to the door. He listened, but heard nothing beyond some indistinguishable mumbling. He glanced in the window, biding his time and giving the attacker a chance to change his own destiny. With the first blow, however, all bets were off, and Race would do whatever was necessary to take the future into his own hands.

Abruptly the sound level inside the room escalated. He only caught snippets, but from what he could gather the woman didn't care for whatever sexual role-play the man had outlined for her. Race shifted so that he could see their images reflected in a mirror inside the room and in the dim light of a single lamp, he saw that the man held a pair of steel handcuffs and what looked like a riding crop.

The woman's eyes flashed as she pointed at the equipment and shook her head vigorously.

Race's gaze still locked on the pair, he slipped the key into the lock. And waited.

"I paid good money for this, bitch, and I expect you to give me my money's worth."

"There's not enough money in the world to get me to do something like that."

"Get on that bed. Now!"

"No way, you twisted son of a bitch."

She turned toward the door, but didn't get far. The man's fist shot out, connecting with her cheek and sending her body sailing. Before the sound of her head thudding against the floor had died away, Race was inside the room.

The door slammed shut and the attacker whirled toward the sound. "What the fuck?"

Race raised the gun and popped off two shots in quick succession.

The first tranquilizer dart hit its mark, lodging firmly in Stephanie's thigh, sedating her and keeping her out of harm's way, as well as making sure she had no recollection of Race's involvement.

The second dart, however, that was intended for the attacker's chest, flew wide.

The moment he'd shifted the barrel toward the man, their eyes had locked, and Race had felt the other man's gaze like a physical blow.

The gun wavered as he staggered backward, coming up against the firm support of the door. Still gripping the gun like a lifeline, he struggled to draw oxygen into starving lungs. He felt paralyzed, pinned, unable to drag his gaze away. The eyes were dark, almost black, yet flat, without depth. Like a black hole that sucked at the soul.

"Who the hell are you?" growled the man. "And what do you want?"

"Get away from her." The words came out as little more than a throaty whisper.

"What are you?" The man's hand reached inside his jacket. "Her boyfriend? Her pimp?"

Race knew he had to act. It took all of his will, but he managed to lift the gun. The effort was weak, and far too slow.

With a roar, the man rushed at Race, slamming him against the door and landing a solid punch to Race's side. Race grunted, but despite the pain that shot through him, in that moment he regained his strength. The man had broken eye contact and Race was freed. With a cry of rage he raised the gun and rammed it against the other man's skull, sending him reeling. A knife glinted in his fingers, and Race realized the true source of the pain in his side. He ignored the warmth that already soaked his shirt and lifted the pistol. He took aim again, but the man recovered too quickly. Before Race could pull the trigger the other man's head rammed into his gut and sent Race careening back into the wall. The force of the blow sent a fresh spear of pain zinging through his side and knocked the breath out of him once again.

The gun slipped from his fingers, but he managed to deflect the man's hand, and avoid another slice of the blade. At the same moment he raised his knee and rammed it into the man's chest.

The man grunted and staggered away.

Race lunged again, reaching for the hand that held the knife, but before he could connect he was stopped by a vicious kick to the side of his neck. His head snapped back and he flew sideways, stumbling further into the room, and tripping over one of Stephanie's outstretched legs. He landed with a thud on the carpet, and before he could recover he heard the click of the lock. He lifted his head just in time to see the man's back as he dashed out the door and fled to his car. Race struggled to his feet, but by the time he made it to the doorway, the car's engine had already roared to life and a moment later the rusted-out Buick was screeching out of the parking lot and on to safety.

Race slouched against the doorframe and pressed a hand to his throbbing side. He checked the wound and determined that it was relatively shallow, slicing through skin and muscle but without penetrating anything vital. It would bleed and leave yet another nasty scar, but beyond that—

"Damn it!" he cursed as the implications of what had just happened hit him.

He turned his gaze on Stephanie, still prone and unmoving. Normally he left the victims where they were, allowing them to awaken and come to their own conclusions as to what had happened. But normally the attacker had been dispatched, the threat eliminated. Not so this time.

What if the man came back looking for her?

Race couldn't leave her. He had to get her to safety, and then he had to take a step back and regroup.

And then he had to figure out what the hell had gone wrong.

Chapter Five

ഇ

Candra was having a very bad day.

Two clients had canceled that day, leaving her with a gaping hole in her afternoon schedule. At first she'd seen it as a bonus, since it gave her a prime opportunity to track down the delinquent Race Kendall who, although he'd resurfaced several days ago, had not yet bothered to call her and make an appointment in order to keep up his end of their bargain.

She knew Race worked out of his home most of the time, so had elected to pay him a personal visit. The trip to his condo, however, had proved futile. He hadn't been home, and when Candra called Megan to ask if she had any ideas on where to find him, she'd informed Candra that Eric had been called out of town for an extended business trip and, as was his habit, he'd asked Race to housesit for him.

No doubt Candra would find him at Eric's—Eric's mansion that was almost an hour's drive away, clear on the other side of the city. Candra had called, but the lack of an answer hadn't deterred her. Megan said that, considering the size of the house, it was very possible Race wouldn't hear the phone. And, of course he might simply decide not to answer, especially if caller ID informed him it was someone he didn't care to talk to.

So, determined to follow through on her commitment to Race, and more than a little curious as to where he'd spent those three days the week before, she'd hit the highway.

As she drove, a storm had rolled in, and the skies had opened up so abruptly that she hadn't had a chance to close the roof on her convertible. The storm had passed quickly, but she had been soaked to the skin and the weather left in the storm's wake was gray and drizzly. And almost as dark as her mood.

Now, her hair hanging in ropy strands about her face, her jeans clinging heavily to every curve, and her white blouse revealing more than she knew was proper, she stood on Eric's stoop and fumed. She'd rung the damn doorbell three times to no avail. She would have assumed Race was out, if not for the presence of his red Mustang in the driveway. He was ignoring her. She didn't like to be ignored.

She tapped her soggy sandal on the concrete step, considering. Perhaps if she went around back… God knew there were enough doors that led into the courtyard. Perhaps one of them had been left unlocked.

She whirled and marched down the steps, following the path around to the back of the house. She rounded the corner and the moment she stepped into the courtyard, realized she wouldn't have to bother jiggling door handles.

Despite the chilly, damp day, Race was in the pool, swimming laps. Naked.

She braced a hand against the stone wall and allowed the anger to seep out of her. She couldn't stay mad if she tried. It was like trying to stay gloomy when presented with a dozen perfect roses, or while basking in the glow of a child's smile. There was an inherent grace and beauty in the lines of his body and the way he moved through the water, and it captivated her. The muscles of his back and arms rippled with each stroke, and his bronzed skin gleamed with moisture. The firm rounds of his buttocks glided just beneath the surface, bunching and relaxing with every kick of his long thighs. She sighed, allowing herself to savor him in a way that she acknowledged was completely unprofessional.

He reached the end of the pool and dived under the surface to change direction. When he resurfaced he had switched from the front crawl to the backstroke, affording her a breathtaking view of his chest and abdomen, and what lay beyond. She allowed her gaze to linger and a smile was just tickling at the corners of her mouth when she caught sight of the flash of white. The pristine bandage stood out starkly against the bronze of his skin, and was just what she needed to jar her out of her reverie.

With a renewed sense of purpose she marched to the side of the pool, and was clearly in his line of vision when he made his next pass.

"You're trespassing," he said, without breaking his stride.

"Eric said I could come anytime. I took him literally."

Race reached the far end and began his next lap, ignoring her.

"Do you always swim in the rain?" she asked.

"I swim when I fucking well feel like swimming." He finished his lap, dove under, but this time when he pushed off he headed directly for her. He grabbed the edge of the pool, just a few inches in front of her feet, and floated there, hair plastered to his scalp, skin gleaming. She wished she could stop noticing—

"What do you want?"

She crouched down. "I want you to live up to our deal."

"Deal. And what deal was that?"

"You know perfectly well what deal, and I refuse to humor you by reciting it again."

He glared at her with that look of his that felt as if it might saw her in two. "Why are you so determined to help someone who doesn't want your help?"

"You want it. You're just having trouble admitting it to yourself. Or maybe to me."

He let out a groan and with a mighty heave, erupted from the water. He strode to a lounge chair and picked up the towel that was draped across it. Rather than wrap it around his waist, however, he draped it around his neck. The white bandage on his side that she'd noticed earlier stood out starkly against his tan. She wanted to ask him about it, but knew now wasn't the time.

"Is Eric paying you to do this?" he asked. "Is that why you're being so stubborn?"

She decided to be honest. "He offered to pay my usual fee, but only *if* you consent to becoming a client. It's not like he's paying me to pester you."

A smile flickered across his lips. "Are you that desperate for clients?"

"Hardly. I turn them away regularly, either because I don't believe I can help them, or because I don't trust their motives. If I was that desperate I wouldn't turn anyone away though, would I?"

"Then why *me*?"

She opened her mouth, but abruptly closed it again. How could she explain it to him when she didn't understand it herself? How could she articulate the draw she felt to him, the ache she felt deep inside whenever she looked into his eyes and caught just a fleeting glimpse of his pain? She couldn't say all that, so she chose not to.

"I want to help you because Megan and Eric are good friends of mine, and they're worried about you. I respect that, and I'm not the kind of person to walk away from someone who so obviously needs my services, and whom I think I can help."

His jaw flexed. "Obviously needs your services. You never did get around to telling me what was so *obvious* about it."

Thunder rumbled in the distance, and the breeze picked up. Candra wrapped her arms around herself and shivered. "Must we do this here?"

"Yes."

She rolled her eyes. "All right. There were a few things, but the one that concerns me the most at this point is that I didn't feel you were an active participant in the lovemaking."

He laughed. "You wanna run that by me again, Doc?"

She pursed her lips, considering. "How do I put this?" There was another crack of thunder, much closer this time. "It felt as if you were…*performing*. As if your only purpose was to please me and make sure I had as many orgasms as possible."

His jaw hardened, and his voice turned defensive. A sure sign that she had hit a nerve. "I recall a pretty intense orgasm on my part. So, how do you figure—"

"It's a hard thing to pin down, but despite the fact that you managed to climax, the session didn't feel mutual. You came, but not because of anything I did. In fact, I got the feeling that my touch made you slightly uncomfortable, but that you allowed it because you knew *I* wanted it."

"That's ridiculous." He whipped the towel off his neck and finally wrapped it around his waist. Before he covered himself, however, she caught a fleeting glimpse of a burgeoning erection, and wondered just when *that* had happened, and why she hadn't noticed it before.

She dragged her gaze back to his face. "I don't think it's ridiculous at all."

"Well, you know, in a way I *was* performing. I was *showing* you what my lovemaking style and technique was like. So, maybe that's absolutely normal."

"It was more than that," she insisted. "Much more."

"So what if I like pleasing the woman I'm with? What's wrong with that? Most women would kill for a man who puts their needs ahead of his own."

Frustrated, she tried a new angle. "You don't allow your partner to consider your needs *at all*." She stepped closer. "Do you?"

He stepped away. "I come. That's all that matters."

"That isn't all that matters. If that was all that mattered you could take care of it yourself. You wouldn't even need a partner."

"I *need* to make her happy. *That's* what I need."

She stepped in closer again, pushing her advantage, and cranking up the pressure. "Come on, Race, you must have needs. All men do. What do you fantasize about? Have you ever shared a fantasy with a partner? Have you ever trusted a woman with that?"

"No. I don't have fantasies."

"Bullshit. Everyone does. If you didn't then I'd really be worried."

His gaze was so hard it twisted her gut. "All right. I have fantasies. I just never shared them with any of my lovers."

"Why not? What stopped you? Didn't you trust them?"

He shook his head, took another step back.

She stepped closer. "Tell me, Race. What stopped you?"

"I didn't want to scare them, okay? I knew that if I told them what my fantasies were it would freak them out. I was afraid they might run away screaming." He turned away from her. "And I couldn't bear for that to happen."

Startled and a little disturbed by his admission, she laid a hand on his arm. "Do you fantasize about hurting women? Is that it?"

He whirled on her. "No. Never. I would never dream of laying a hand on a woman in violence. And I despise any man who does."

"Then tell me, Race, and I promise I won't be shocked or scared. You've got to believe me when I tell you I've pretty much heard it all. There isn't much left."

His gaze remained skeptical.

"Tell me and I promise I won't judge you. And I won't leave."

He shook his head slowly. "I don't know."

"Perhaps I could help you live out your fantasy. It wouldn't be the first time I've done that, and I know from experience that it can be very therapeutic. It would be therapeutic for you to allow someone else to please you for a change, to focus on your needs, and learn how to share something very personal. Depending on what it is, I'd be perfectly willing to try. But you have to tell me."

The clouds opened and raindrops pelted their skin. Race was putting on a good show, but she could see goose bumps form on his arms.

She said, "Let's go inside and discuss it. Tell me what you dream of when you're alone at night, and maybe, just maybe, we can make that dream come true." She grasped his hand and squeezed. "Together."

With a sigh of resignation, he nodded. Her hand gripped firmly in his, he led her inside, out of the rain, and deep into the sanctuary of the house.

* * * * *

Race stood on the bearskin rug in the penthouse bedroom that he had claimed for his own. They'd turned the fire on low to take the dampness out of the air, and to keep

Race from getting a chill as Candra spread oil over every inch of his nude body.

He closed his eyes and allowed himself to enjoy her touch. Her hands were gentle but firm as she smoothed the patchouli-scented oil over his back and shoulders and down his arms. She paused occasionally, tracing a ridge of muscle, or a thread of sinew, gleaning obvious enjoyment from the exploration of his body. He took pleasure from that, almost as much as from the touch of her hands, and the anticipation of what was to come. Of what they were preparing for.

She had listened attentively as he outlined his fantasy. He had explained it in detail, listing every item without inflection or emotion, maintaining a mask that gave away no hint of the turmoil within.

To his relief and surprise she hadn't seemed the least bit unnerved by his requests, taking it all in stride and asking questions only when necessary to clarify some ambiguous point. He couldn't help wondering what the therapist in her read in his words, but he decided not to worry about that. He'd dreamed of this, wondered about it for years. He didn't know where the thoughts and ideas had come from, but they had been vivid in his mind for a very long time. He'd run through the fantasy numerous times, hoping that somehow it might lessen some of the intense, unidentifiable pressure he felt deep inside. That it might ease the ache he felt whenever he was with a woman he cared about. But the fantasy, no matter how intense, had been inadequate.

He had a chance now to explore the reality with a woman that he found beautiful and intensely exciting. His response to her last week, and then his erection that afternoon at the pool when he'd allowed himself to notice the way her wet clothes clung to her body, were testament to just how attractive he found her.

This was a golden opportunity and he wasn't about to let it slip through his fingers.

He opened his eyes.

She was behind him now but he could see her reflection clearly in the mirror on the far side of the room. Her hair had dried, and cascaded to her shoulders in a rich, mahogany wave. Her body was lean and lithe, her movements economical yet graceful. He would hardly have needed the embellishment, but the black thong and lace bra she wore were more than enough to keep his cock at full attention.

She stopped for a moment to add a fresh dollop of oil to her palm before returning to her task. Her hands rubbed over the small of his back and he felt himself tense reflexively when she reached his buttocks.

"Shh." She skimmed over the curve of muscle, leaving a film of sweet oil and a vague tingling on his skin. "You have to relax. You have to trust me." Her fingers slipped into the crease and he willed his muscles to yield, allowing her to penetrate deeper, to spread the oil where it would be needed the most. She reached the sensitive skin of his anus and massaged it lightly.

"That's better. Now I just need you to bend forward a little…" Her voice was dark and soft like chocolate that's been left out in the sun, and it soothed his nerves. He did as she asked.

"Good." Her oil-slicked fingers penetrated him and massaged the lubricant deep inside.

He took a deep breath and blew it out.

She reached deeper still. "Oh yes. That's very good." She withdrew and penetrated again. "How does that feel?"

"Mm."

"Do you want more?" Her other hand came around to cup his balls, her thumb stroked his cock.

73

He was tempted, but he shook his head. "No," he breathed. "Not like this."

"All right." He couldn't be sure, but he thought she sounded vaguely disappointed. "Whatever you want." She withdrew and dipped her hands in a basin of warm water that she had brought out, quickly washing her hands before reaching for the oil again.

She stood in front of him, poured a dollop into her palm and rubbed her hands together. She smoothed the oil over his chest and down his abdomen, but at his bandage she hesitated.

She touched it tentatively. "May I take this off?"

"Yes. That's a waterproof dressing, and there's another surgical dressing underneath. But it's much smaller and easier to avoid."

She reached for the tape and began to peel it away. "What if the oil takes off the surgical tape?"

"I don't think it'll matter. The wound is more than a week old, and it has stitches, so—"

He winced as she ripped away the last piece of tape.

She looked up at him. "What happened, Race? What kind of injury is it?"

"Just a little cut I got because I wasn't watching where I was going. Nothing to worry about."

He could see in her eyes that she didn't believe him, but he had no intention of telling her the truth.

She nodded and finished massaging the oil into the skin of his belly and sides before continuing lower. She left no part untouched, paying particular attention to his cock and balls, laying down the oil in long, silky strokes and massaging it in deeply. He had to grit his teeth and clench his fists in an effort to stay still and control his reaction to her.

"Finished," she said at last. She stepped back, raked her eyes over him, and let out a long, low whistle.

"What?"

"Bathed in firelight, with your body covered with oil, you do make a picture, Mr. Kendall. It's enough to give a girl the vapors."

Despite himself he laughed. "Somehow you and *the vapors* don't quite go together."

Ironically, she lost her smile. "You should smile more, Race. That smile can melt hearts."

He hardened his expression, and chose not to acknowledge the comment. "Shall we head downstairs?"

"You're sure about this?"

"Why? Do *you* want to back out?"

"No. I just want to make sure it's what you want."

He reached for the pair of plush terrycloth robes and held one out to her. "It is."

She accepted the robe and slipped it on. "All right, then. Let's go."

Candra followed Race in silence. They descended the stairs past the second floor, to the first, through the main living quarters to a small room tucked away in an alcove just off the entrance. The tiny room was dim. It had no windows, lit only by a pair of lamps that hung on either side of a carved oak door on the far wall. The lamps hung from the mouths of carved gargoyles that resembled dogs, their lips curled in a snarl, fangs bared in warning. Their eyes glinted with something disturbing.

Already at the door, Race pulled a key from his pocket and fitted it into the lock. When the door swung open,

Candra hung back, her eyes glued to the pair guarding the entrance to their domain.

Race followed her gaze. "Don't worry about them. They're just figments of Eric's twisted imagination. He wants people to think twice before violating his inner sanctum."

She swallowed, pressed a hand to the flesh that peeked out between the lapels of her robe. "If that's his purpose he's succeeded."

A smile flickered across his lips. "Honey, you ain't seen nothin' yet."

And then he led her on.

The staircase was dimly lit, steep and narrow. The steps felt cold against her bare feet, hard and slick like damp slate, and yet her feet didn't slip. She trailed a finger along the wall to her left and sensed the same mysterious material. They stepped off the last stair and found themselves at the end of a long narrow hallway lined with half a dozen doors, three on each side. A flickering electric torch marked each entrance, and illuminated the gargoyle that identified that particular room. Unicorns and fairies mingled with dragons and mermaids.

"These are *all* fetish rooms?" she asked as he led her toward the far end. Race had told her of Eric's secret stash of sex toys and fantasy paraphernalia, but she hadn't grasped the sheer scope of it all.

"He prefers to call them 'theme rooms' and yes, he has six of them." He stopped at a door marked by particularly fierce dragon. "So far."

She shook her head in wonder. "I knew Eric had a reputation as something of a ladies' man, but this?" She blew out a slow breath. "I had no idea."

"Eric's parties are quite renowned among a certain...segment of the population. People vie for invitations, crawl over each other for a chance to come here, and these rooms are a big part of the reason."

She blinked. "You mean, the other night. When we were here…"

He nodded. "These rooms were in full swing by the time you arrived."

"But how—"

"Any guests who are interested give him their watch or a ring, or some other personal item when they arrive, and at a designated time he takes all the participants into his office and makes a draw. He draws the items at random though so you take your chances. He tries to make sure there's a male-female couple in each room, but there's certainly no guarantee you'll end up with the person you arrived with. And he might even decide to add a third or even a fourth into the mix, so you never know who you'll end up with. Or where. But you abide by the draw or you're asked to leave the premises." He placed his hand on the knob. "And forget about another invitation. One chance is all you get."

She drew in a deep breath, tried to assimilate it all. "Megan. Does she know?"

He just stared at her, unblinking, but even as she asked the question she had figured it out. Megan knew. And she hated it.

"How about you, Race? Have you ever participated?"

He seemed to consider that for a moment and then, abruptly, he pushed open the door and stepped across the threshold. "I helped him design this room."

The fact that he hadn't exactly answered the question didn't escape her, but her curiosity was soon overshadowed by awe. She stepped inside, directly into the heart of a medieval dungeon.

Torches flickered and light from an enormous fireplace licked at the walls and cast eerie shadows.

It was cool, but although the floors and walls were all made of the same mysterious material that mimicked slate, the room lacked the cold, bone-damp feeling one normally associated with an underground cavern. She did shiver, however, when she caught sight of the accessories that adorned the walls.

Manacles and thumbscrews, whips and chains, knives and picks of various sizes and descriptions hung from a series of hooks around the room. The chamber echoed with drips of water and she thought she heard the distant scream of a woman.

She turned a questioning gaze on Race who had shed his robe and now stood naked before the centerpiece of the room. It resembled a rack, but there the similarity ended. Race had told her in detail how it had been modified to suit Eric's playful purpose.

Race's smile was incongruous with the surroundings. "Sound effects add to the ambiance, don't you think? You might even hear a bat flutter by if you listen really closely." He nodded toward the instruments hanging from the walls. "And don't worry, those are just for show. The real toys are in that cupboard on the far wall. There's also more oil in case we need it."

She turned to see the rough-hewn wooden cabinet in the corner behind her. "Okay. Let's get started." Ignoring the subtle edge in his voice and the flutter in her own gut, she shrugged off her robe, walked to the cupboard and flung it open. She surveyed the contents—an assortment of vibrators and dildos, harnesses, leather gloves, handcuffs and floggers. She glanced over her shoulder, found him glaring at her. "Well, get into position. I'll be over to lock you in in a minute."

He crossed his arms, causing his pecs to ripple, his biceps to bulge. "I don't know about this. I've changed my mind."

She chose a long latex flogger that resembled a cat-o'-nine-tails. She slapped it once against her bare palm, winced at the surprising sting. The soft whip had bite but wouldn't draw blood regardless of how long or hard it was used. The oil on his body would also serve to protect his sensitive skin while still allowing him to experience the full effect. To feel the pain that, for whatever reason, he seemed to crave.

She had decided quite quickly that this exercise wasn't about domination, as he certainly wasn't a submissive. This was about something else entirely, and the only way to identify that something was to work through his fantasy and see what they found on the other side.

Slowly she turned around, immersing herself into the character he'd asked her to become, burying her instincts and plunging herself into the game. "I don't really care if you've changed your mind, do I? Now do as I say."

"No."

She hardened her gaze and strode over to him. "I don't tolerate backtalk."

"Fucking bitch."

She slapped him. The echo of her open palm connecting with his cheek echoed through the cavernous room and sent vibrations zinging up her arm. Other than a momentary flicker of his eyes and the set of his jaw he didn't react.

She kept her voice low and firm. "Do it." And without warning she drew back the whip and laid the lash across his buttocks.

He winced but remained immobile.

She lashed him again, harder, across his back this time.

A muscle twitched in his jaw but this time he turned around and moved closer to the rack which had been tilted upright to facilitate access. He needed only to step into the complex metal frame and Candra would be able to adjust the bonds for his size and then lock him in, all while he remained standing.

"Back in," she instructed. "I want you facing me."

His brows knit in confusion and she could almost see the retort form on his tongue. She wasn't sticking to his plan, but apparently he decided to remain in character and allow her to take control. He kept his objections to himself.

Remaining silently stoic, he backed into the rack and waited patiently as she adjusted the bonds for his height and locked him in. Metal cuffs lined with velvet bound his wrists and ankles, and a leather strap banded his chest.

She stepped back, surveyed him. "Good. That'll do nicely."

"I don't see how this will—"

The snap of the flogger across his abdomen shut him up well enough. "Quiet." She trailed the latex tails across his belly and down over his cock that had only now begun to thicken. "And let me admire you."

She tucked the flogger under her arm and stepped closer, close enough to smell the patchouli-scented oil mixed with his own musk. She skimmed her fingers over his chest, brushed a thumb across his nipple. "God, you're beautiful." She leaned in, cupping his balls with her hand as she drew a lazy circle around his nipple with her tongue. "Tasty, too." She glanced up to find him looking down at her, watching her with that slice-to-the-heart gaze of his.

She frowned, stepped back. "I don't like the way you're looking at me."

His jaw flexed, but his eyes never wavered.

She decided his gaze was as insolent as his words—if not more so. "If that's the way it's going to be…" She spun on her heel and walked back to the cabinet, began rummaging through it. She found what she was looking for, decided it wasn't enough, and kept looking until she found the second item. She walked back to him with the two items dangling provocatively from her fingers.

"A blindfold? What the—"

She laid the flogger soundly across his belly, watched him wince. "I *told you* to be quiet."

When his mouth seemed to be firmly closed she reached up and slid the black velvet blindfold into place. "If you can't tame that 'fuck you' stare of yours I'll just have to do it for you. Now open your mouth."

"Fuck y—"

She slipped the gag between his teeth and interrupted his tirade before it started. He shook his head in an effort to dislodge it, but her hands were too quick and too firm. She pulled it in snug and knotted it tightly behind his head.

"Better." She drew a hand across his abdomen, brushed her fingertips down the length of his cock. She wrapped her hand around it and squeezed, stroking the tip with her thumb and enjoying the thrum of his pulse against her palm. His erection filled her hand, even as his muscles twitched with what she was sure was the urge to push her away. "Much better."

She stroked his balls, leaned down and teased his cock with her tongue. "You hate this, don't you?" She wrapped her lips around him, sucked, drew away. "You hate giving up control, receiving pleasure."

His biceps twitched, legs jerked.

She took him into her mouth again, drew her lips down the length of him, massaged his balls. She watched him writhe against her touch even as his arousal increased. She tasted the first beads of cum, lapped at them with her tongue.

"Mmm." She dug her fingers into the muscles of his ass to hold him tight, heard the soft thud as the flogger fell to the floor. "This isn't what you wanted, is it?" She sucked him again. "You wanted me to take you forcibly, but not like this, right?"

He groaned as she took him deeply into her throat, sucked him hard, pulled away.

"Well, that's all well and good but I'm in charge and we're going to do this my way." She tickled the tip of his cock with her tongue.

He shook his head, fighting it.

And then she attacked him with her mouth. She gripped his ass and raked her lips and teeth over him with a fierce abandon that made her own pulse throb. He twisted against his bindings and she felt his sweat collect beneath her hands. His breath quickened and he groaned as he began to give himself over to her will.

And then she stopped.

Her mouth abandoned his rock-hard cock, left him panting and wanting as she stepped back and reached for the remote control for the rack.

"That was good for a start." She hit the button and watched as the motor whirred to life and the unit began to recline. "But we're not nearly done."

She stopped only when he was completely horizontal, his cock jutting upward, damp and throbbing.

She surveyed him. Bound, blindfolded and gagged, gleaming with oil and sweat he presented a picture that was at once exciting and disturbing. Erotic and unsettling. She ignored the ball of undefined emotion that had knotted in her gut, and picked up the flogger.

She stepped closer and trailed the latex strands down his gleaming belly, across his straining cock. "You want me to use this thing, don't you? Punish you."

He nodded.

For what? she wondered, but knew that question would have to be answered later.

"I want that, too," she breathed. "But not yet. Right now I want something else altogether."

She dropped the flogger and slipped off her panties. She climbed onto the rack, straddling him, her knees resting on the pair of pads that had been built into the unit for that very purpose. She poised herself over him, grasped his cock and tickled her pussy with it. "Feel that?" she asked. "Do you want it?"

He shook his head, playing the game.

"Of course you do. You want exactly what I tell you to want." She held her breath as she lowered herself over him, sheathed herself around him, let him fill her. "Mmm. That's it."

She began to pump her hips, stroking herself over him as she massaged her clit in counterpoint to her own movements. His cock throbbed and he writhed against her, even as his own body demanded he respond. His hips began to thrust in time to her rhythm, and a series of low groans rumbled in his throat.

She braced her hands against his chest and leaned forward, accelerated her movements. "Don't come," she commanded, even as she felt her own climax approaching. "Whatever you do..." She ground out the words between frantic breaths that sought desperately for oxygen. "Don't. Come."

The wave swelled within her, burst over her, quick and hard. She ground herself against him and allowed the orgasm to ravage her even as she continued pummeling him with her body. His face contorted as she pulsed around him and he fought his own climax.

She continued to move over him, to torture him with his own pleasure. Despite her breathlessness, she steeled her voice. "Don't, Race. You need to control yourself. Whatever you do, don't—"

His body arched and he let out a long, low moan as he climaxed, pumping himself into her and conceding defeat.

When it was done she leaned down and reached around to untie the gag. She pulled the damp material from his mouth and languished a long, hot kiss on his lips.

"Ah, Race," she whispered over the sound of his rasping breath, "now you've done it. You didn't listen, so now I really will have to punish you." She drew his lower lip between her teeth. "Won't I?"

Chapter Six

🕉

"There." Candra dropped the remote control and reached for the flogger that she'd set on a small table beside the other toys she'd pulled from the cupboard. "Comfy?"

He said nothing, but she could see from the ripple of muscles across his back, that he was anything but. He now lay facedown in the rack, tilted at a slight angle that gave her easier access to his body. She'd decided not to replace the gag, but the blindfold remained. In this position his gaze no longer bothered her, but he'd asked her to remove it. So, of course, she'd refused.

Despite his protests that it was unnecessary, she'd also replenished the coating of oil, had taken great pleasure in spreading it over every inch of available skin and in feeling his muscles turn to liquid beneath her hands.

The relaxed state, however, was due to come to an end.

Without warning, she drew back her hand and snapped the flogger across his buttocks.

His body jerked, most likely from surprise rather than pain. The discomfort, however, would come. She laid down a blow across his lower back. His shoulders.

She paused. "You owe me an apology. Let's hear it."

"I owe you nothing."

The flogger snapped against his skin, harder this time, and she noted that it had begun to turn pink. "You called me a name." She hit him again. "And disobeyed me." Again. "For that you need to apologize."

"No."

The sound of the whip echoed through the cavern and made her gut churn. "Does it hurt yet? Do you want me to stop?"

"Yes. It hurts." His voice had taken on a haunting tone that shivered over her skin.

"Then tell me to stop. Beg me."

His hands twisted against the restraints. "Let me the hell outta here." That wasn't the safe phrase he'd chosen. He'd been adamant that she stop when, and only when, he used a very specific phrase.

The strips of latex nipped at his skin and he jerked, from pain perhaps this time. Her arm began to feel heavy. "Apologize and I will."

He shook his head, tried to twist his body. "Fuck you!"

She paused, her arm drawn back ready for another blow. "What did you say?"

"I said fuck you. Go fuck yourself and while you're at it let me go!" The rack rattled with his attempts to loosen his bonds.

Resigning herself to the inevitable, she walked to the table and laid down the flogger. She heaved an exaggerated sigh. "You leave me no alternative." She picked up the vibrating dildo that had already been slicked with oil, and strapped it to herself. She'd worn one once before, and the experience had been very memorable. Very…unique. It couldn't compare to this.

She walked over to him and flipped the switch to activate the vibrator. She'd opted for a unit without a clitoral stimulator, knowing she needed all her concentration focused on him.

He twisted his head, searching for the source of the sound. "What's that? What are you doing?"

She placed her hands on the small of his back and slid them down over his buttocks. "Teaching you a lesson, of course." Slipped her fingers into the crease of his ass and guided the dildo into position. She felt him tense.

"Fight me and this will just be that much harder."

"Don't," was his only protest. "Please don't." Again his voice had taken on that haunting edge that curled in her gut.

"Do you want to apologize now?" she asked, even as the tip of the dildo pressed against the sensitive tissue of his anus.

His hands twisted and he tried in vain to shift away. "Just let me go. Just—"

She penetrated him. She had to use more force than she intended just because he was fighting her so hard, and she was afraid she'd really hurt him.

But then when she eased in a little further his muscles seemed to relax, and it became easier.

"See?" she taunted, withdrawing and thrusting slowly again. "You want it. I knew you did."

"No." He groaned. "Please."

She thrust again.

"Stop."

Sweat beaded on his back and his hands clenched into fists.

She continued, slipping her hands around his waist both to anchor herself to him and to fondle his erection. He was rock-hard and his excitement aroused her.

She accelerated the thrusts, felt him give a little more of himself to her.

"Jesus," he breathed. "Sweet Jesus. Why are you doing this?"

She paused, the dildo buried deep inside him, the vibrations coursing through both of them.

He groaned, tried to shift his hips away. She followed.

"Apologize."

His breathing was becoming ragged, sweat dripped from his hair. "Fuck." He sucked in a breath. "You. Let me out."

She withdrew and thrust again, harder, faster. "Apologize, damn you!"

She touched his cock and his pulse against her palm felt like the beat of a war drum.

He tensed, the climax building in him.

"Help me," he rasped, his voice faint but earnest.

The words startled her, confused her, but she only hesitated a moment because he shifted his hips, this time in search of more.

"Somebody…" He groaned. "Somebody please…"

She thrust deep, held it there and squeezed his cock.

"Help me!" the words ripped from his throat, even as the orgasm tore from his body. He arched his back, jerked and spasmed, letting out a cry and pumping his seed onto the floor until he was dry, and until at last he moaned the words she'd been waiting to hear.

"I'm sorry." The whispered words were so quiet, so desperate, a plea that raked across her heart. "I'm so, so, sorry."

He relaxed, his body suddenly boneless as he sagged against his bindings. Slightly alarmed, she rushed to withdraw from him, dropped the harness to the floor and quickly unsnapped the restraints. She grasped his elbow and, supporting him, urged him to step away from the rack and sit down on a small wooden stool beside the table.

He sank down onto it gratefully.

"Race?" she asked, slipping off the blindfold. "Race, are you all right?"

He shook his head and turned away.

The tears that stained his eyes and shimmered on his cheeks, however, were answer enough.

Race sat on the stool, only vaguely aware of the chamber and Candra's presence. Instead he found himself sitting on his mother's bed in a small, dingy apartment overlooking the city…

* * * * *

"Race, are you watching television?"

"Uh…kinda."

Nine-year-old Race shifted a little closer to the television and turned up the volume. He'd turned it way down low in the hopes that she wouldn't hear it and would think he was reading the book she'd brought home from the library. He supposed there was no point in straining his ears now.

He looked up to see his mother glaring at him from the doorway to her bedroom. "Just five more minutes, Mommy?"

"The television in here is for Mommy to watch the news at night, not to provide you with a secret place to watch your shoot-'em-up cartoons."

"It's just Bugs Bunny, Mom. Can't I just finish watching this one?" He turned on his thousand-watt smile and gave her his best puppy-dog eyes. "Pleeease?"

She rolled her eyes and laughed even as she strode across the room and switched off the TV. "Someday that smile is going to have women swooning at your feet but it won't work on me, young man."

"Eww, girls. I'll never like 'em."

She grabbed his hand and led him from the room. "You like me, don't you?"

"You're not a girl, you're a mom."

"Hmm." She stopped and pointed at the battered old Steinway piano that sat in the corner of their living room. "Just for that you're going to have to practice an extra fifteen minutes."

His shoulders slouched. His mom had two obsessions, two things that she always nagged him about—books and piano lessons. Of the two he preferred the piano, but even that ran a distant second to chocolate chip cookies and cartoons. "Can't I practice later, Mom? After supper?"

He could smell the hamburgers frying and his stomach was already doing flip-flops in anticipation.

"You can do fifteen minutes now, and fifteen minutes after supper."

He hoisted himself onto the bench, stared at the book that sat open on the ledge, and made a sour face. "Do I *have* to? I'll never be good enough to play at…" He frowned. "What's that place called again?"

"Carnegie Hall."

"Yeah. I'll never play there. I don't wanna, anyway."

When she didn't say anything he looked up at her, and was surprised to see tears swelling in her eyes.

She brushed them away, knelt down beside him and grasped his hands. "I know that, honey. When your teacher said that she was just trying to encourage you because she knows you're very talented and have a lot of potential. But even though I know that you'll probably never be a concert pianist, and you'll probably never write the great Canadian novel, I want you to practice and read every day. I want you to work hard and do your best."

"Why? Who cares if I play piano? What's the point?"

"The point is that it makes you a better person. Music and books and art are all important because..." She made an odd little sound in her throat, then reached up to brush a strand of hair from his eyes. "The point is that you're going to learn things that I never learned, and go places I never went. You're going to grow up and go to college and have a successful career. You're going to have a good life, and a family and people who love you. And music and reading are just a small part of that, but they're both a step in the right direction."

He frowned. "Huh?"

She smiled, her eyes twinkling mirrors of his own. "For now just do it because I said so." She ruffled his hair. "And because I'll get you an ice-cream cone after your lesson tomorrow if you impress your teacher with your scales."

His hopes soared. "Really?"

"Really."

"Chocolate chip cookie dough?"

"You bet. Now —"

The banging on the door was so loud it made Race's tummy rattle.

"Janine!" yelled a man's voice. "I know you're in there, now answer the damn door, you slut!"

His mother erupted to her feet and stared at the door. The fear in her eyes twisted through Race like a snake. He jumped off the bench and grabbed her hand. "What is it, Mommy? Is it Danny?"

Danny was the man his mom worked for, and sometimes he talked loud and got drunk but Race had never seen his mom act like it scared her. She always told Race that he talked mean, but he meant well. She said that he treated all his girls pretty good, all things considered, and that he tried hard to keep them safe.

She squeezed his hand. "No, honey. It isn't Danny."

"Should we call him? I know his number. I could call."

"Danny's out of town tonight."

"Janine!" The pounding grew louder. "Open this goddamn door before I break it down."

She began dragging Race toward his bedroom. "Just a minute!" she cried. "I'm just getting dressed!"

"Why bother? It's not like I haven't seen that cunt of yours before!"

"Mommy?" Race's eyes filled with tears, both of terror and confusion. "What's going on?"

She opened his closet door and shoved him inside. "I'll explain later, but right now I need you to stay in here and stay quiet!" She started to close the door but he reached out and grabbed her hand. "Let me help, Mom. I can help. I can protect you just like Danny can."

She looked down at him, blinked, and then with the pounding on the door echoing in his ears she said, "No, honey. It's *my* job to protect you. You're all that matters. You're everything." She pressed a kiss to his forehead. "Now listen to me. No matter what happens…no matter what you hear or see, I want you to stay in here. Crouch down in the dark and stay very still and very quiet. No matter what happens don't come out." She squeezed his hand, held his gaze. "Promise me."

Tears dripping from his chin, he nodded. "I promise."

"Good." She stepped back and started to close the slatted closet door.

"I love you, Mommy!"

The door clicked shut. "I love you, too."

And then she went to open the door…

The memories spun through Race's mind, inexorably intertwined with the emotions that accompanied them.

Rage. Embarrassment. Horror. Grief. Shame. And a mountain range of guilt.

Awakened from decades of slumber, the emotions swirled through him like ancient ghosts that had taken on gruesome new form. Instead of exorcizing his demons, the session with Candra had given them new life. They'd sprouted claws and fangs, and seemed intent on stripping him of flesh, consuming his humanity.

His body had taken pleasure from what Candra had done, had responded to her in ways he hadn't anticipated, had never intended. He'd tried to control his responses but he may as well have tried to stop himself from sweating. This fantasy wasn't supposed to be about pleasure, at least not about physical pleasure. It was supposed to be about paying dues and purging demons, about gaining some understanding of the pain and humiliation his mother had experienced. The sting of physical pain, the humiliation of having one's body sexually violated, the fear and helplessness that came of not knowing what would come— these were the things he'd wanted to experience, things he needed to understand. But it hadn't turned out that way. He'd felt some discomfort, certainly, but instead of diminishing his excitement it had heightened it. And being bound and subject to Candra's will had only exaggerated the effect.

Of course a latex flogger and a strap-on dildo were inadequate substitutes. He'd known it was all an illusion, had known it was a game and that he could stop it at any time with but a word. Only at the very end had he lost himself in the fantasy, the moment intense but far too brief to be meaningful.

He was never in any real danger, never experienced real pain, and therein lay the problem. But he knew he couldn't take it to that next level, and couldn't help wondering if that meant he was too weak. Or too strong.

Either way, instead of feeling lighter, he felt weighed down by all the old emotions, now coupled with a fresh, raw guilt, a brand-new shame. He'd taken physical pleasure, achieved orgasm and release in something that was intended to represent discipline and, yes, punishment. Where did he go from here? he wondered. How did he step into the future when he was still so mired in the past?

He felt Candra's hand on his elbow as she urged him to stand and settled the robe on his shoulders. She took his hand and led him from the room, down the hallway and up the stairs. She murmured questions and what he assumed were words of comfort, but he barely heard them, barely felt the warmth of her flesh against his palm. He was too lost in his memories.

* * * * *

Candra poured a healthy dose of brandy into a snifter and swirled it in her palm to warm it. Her eyes rested on the grand piano that gleamed in the corner of Eric's study. She longed to hear Race play again, but knew her wish was not likely to be fulfilled. At least not tonight.

She crossed to the other side of the room, stood behind the deep leather chair where he sat, huddled, wrapped in the thick terrycloth robe, staring out into the stormy July evening. Rain continued to pelt the stained glass doors and the echo of retreating thunder rumbled in the distance.

She rounded the chair and kneeled in front of him, offered him the snifter. "Take this."

He shook his head, pulled the robe a little tighter.

She rested a hand on his knee and saw him wince at the contact.

She didn't remove her hand. "Just drink a little. Please. It'll make you feel better."

"It doesn't work." His eyes closed for a moment, the misery on his face plain. "God knows I've tried that. I've tried everything."

She took his hand, pressed the snifter into his palm. "This isn't an escape. It's just to help you relax so you can tell me what all that was about downstairs."

He looked at her then, for perhaps the first time since they'd left his fantasy. His gaze was dull now, lacking its usual cutting edge, its usual chill. "It doesn't matter. It didn't work."

He sipped from the brandy, closed his eyes as his throat muscles worked and the alcohol did its work.

He stared into the depths of the snifter. "I guess I always knew it wouldn't, but I hoped. I should learn not to bother."

"Not to bother hoping?"

He took another sip, said nothing.

"Hope is essential, Race. You lose hope, you stop living."

"I stopped living twenty-five years ago. I've just been existing ever since."

Emotions knotted in her throat, stung the backs of her eyes. "Since your mother died."

His gaze registered surprise. "How—"

"Eric told me. He told me about the accident and about how you had to sit by and watch her die."

He stared at her, his eyes wide and unblinking, and then, to her shock, he let his head fall back onto the high leather back, and he laughed.

It was brief, the laughter tight, strangled. "Oh Christ," he said, wiping tears from his eyes. "That's a good one. I had forgotten about that."

She blinked in confusion. "Forgotten? Forgotten about watching your mother die?"

"No," he said, his voice suddenly hard. "I could never forget that."

"Then maybe you should talk about it. I really think you need—"

Abruptly he stood, the movement upsetting her balance and almost sending her sprawling. He walked to the bar as she scrambled to her feet.

He topped up his snifter. "I don't want to talk about this."

"You have to."

"Like hell I do." He tipped the glass and drained half of it.

"You experienced something very traumatic, Race. I know it was a long time ago, but time doesn't necessarily heal all wounds. The only way to deal with it is to face it, and what we did downstairs may be a step in that direction, but it's not enough."

"You have no idea what I faced back then. What I have to face now. Every day. Every goddamn fucking *day*!" Suddenly he raised his arm and hurled the brandy glass across the room, watched it shatter against the stone hearth, then turned his bleary gaze on Candra.

She moved over to him and grasped his hand. It felt cold so she pressed it between her palms to warm it. "You're right. I don't know, but I want to. I want to hear everything, and I think you need to tell me."

He took a deep breath, his gaze focused on his hand held in hers. "It wasn't a car accident."

"It wasn't?"

He shook his head.

His hand held firmly in hers she led him to the wide leather couch that faced the fireplace. She urged him down into the corner, tucked a blanket around him and settled herself beside him. "So, what was it? How did she die?"

He pressed the heels of his hands against his eyes. "Christ."

"Do you remember it? Perhaps you've blocked some of it out."

His hands fell in his lap. "No. I remember. I remember enough."

He stared at his hands, and when he made no move to say more she prompted him. "How old were you?"

He took a deep breath, fortifying himself. "Nine. Or almost nine. My birthday was in two weeks and I had asked if I could have a party. My first real party with friends and a cake and everything."

Because she thought he needed the contact she stroked his hand. "Why had you never had a party before?"

"We had always moved around so much, I never had time to make friends. We'd been in Vancouver almost two years, and it was the first time I knew anyone well enough to invite them over."

"Where had you lived before?"

"Edmonton, Calgary, Winnipeg. We'd been working our way west from Toronto ever since I was a baby. She'd always get nervous when we stayed somewhere too long because she was afraid he'd find her." He rubbed his temple and then returned his hand to his lap, where she laid hers over it once again. "Before you have to ask, *he* was the pimp she'd had in Toronto."

Candra felt a little jolt of shock which quickly melted into sympathy. The news surprised her and yet she thought perhaps it shouldn't have. She wasn't sure why, but she thought maybe she should have guessed.

He continued. "I don't know much about it except snippets that I caught when I overheard her talking to the other girls. But from what I gather she ran away from home really young, and hooked up with this guy on the streets. He was a possessive, cruel, sadistic son of a bitch, and he beat her regularly. It took her getting pregnant with me to make her desperate enough to run away, but he had always warned her that he'd find her if she ever left." He turned his hand over so that their palms met, the gesture so casual as to be almost absent. "She was right to worry."

"So he found her."

He nodded.

"And he killed her."

His fingers curled around hers and squeezed, hard enough that it verged on painful, but she didn't pull away. Couldn't bear to.

"He didn't just kill her, Candra. He beat her and raped her and then he slit her throat and watched her bleed to death." His next words chilled her blood. "And I saw everything. It was filtered through the slats of an old closet door, but I saw it just the same." He let go of her hand, and rose from the couch. Returning to the French doors, he stared out through the multicolored glass into blackness. "And I did nothing. I sat in there and hugged my knees and cried, and watched as this…this…monster defiled and murdered my mother. And I did nothing to stop it."

Candra stood beside him. "She put you in there to protect you, didn't she?"

"Of course."

"So you did the right thing."

He whirled on her, his gaze fierce. *"The right thing*? I stood by and watched my mother die. How the hell can that be the right thing?"

Despite the fire in his eyes and the rage in his voice she didn't step back. "It was the right thing because it was exactly what she told you to do, wasn't it? Her first concern was protecting you."

He opened his mouth to speak, but then abruptly closed it again. He shook his head and stalked back to the couch, sat down and dropped his head into his hands. "It was the closet in my room, and I'm sure she put me in there because she thought it was safer. She probably thought she could quiet him down with sex, or take a beating, but that she could keep him in the living room or her bedroom."

Suddenly he looked up. "She never brought tricks home. She protected me from that. I wouldn't want you to think—"

She laid a hand on his shoulder. "I never thought otherwise."

He nodded, swallowed. "But he saw something in the living room that clued him in to the fact that she had a kid, so he came looking."

"What did she tell him?"

"She told him I was at a friend's house or something. Convinced him I wasn't there, but they were standing in my room arguing about it and when she told him to get the hell out that really pissed him off and he hit her. She fell on the bed and he..." His voice trailed off, and he rubbed a hand across his eyes.

"He decided that was as good a place as any to teach her a lesson."

He nodded, sat back and blew out a long, slow breath. "Yeah. I guess he did."

"Can you tell me what you saw, Race? Can you tell me how it made you feel?"

Race stared at her, his mind trying to grapple with what she was asking of him.

What did he see that day? What did he feel? She was asking him to recall things he'd spent twenty-five years trying to forget. Despite his efforts, however, sometimes the images were so vivid they seared his eyelids, the sounds so intense he had to cover his ears to block them out. Certainly he remembered, but he never remembered intentionally. And he never, *ever* talked about it.

"Race." She picked up his hand, cradled it in her own. "It's the only way."

He was surprised to realize how inviting her touch had become, to find his fingers curling into hers. "I remember the sounds more than anything else."

"The sounds?"

"Yes. I think maybe it's because I closed my eyes at first. When she hit the mattress and I saw blood on her mouth it scared me so badly I closed my eyes. I couldn't bear to watch, but then the sounds became enhanced somehow, clearer. More vivid." He'd heard the thud of flesh on flesh, the crack of bone. His mother's labored breathing and the cries for help she tried so hard to suppress. And he'd heard the words the man had said, filthy, ugly words about his mother. About the bastard child she'd given birth to.

"And then I thought it wasn't right for me to hide my eyes from what was happening. I thought I should watch. I thought I owed her that."

She squeezed his hand, the warmth of her touch the only thing anchoring him to the present.

He continued. "But I was so scared that when I finally made myself open my eyes, I focused only on her, on her face. Her eyes. She was lying on the bed then, with him holding her down. I think she was naked, and he must have been raping her at that point but I didn't understand that then. All I knew was that she seemed to be looking right at me. There was blood on her face, and one eye was all puffed up, but she'd turned her head to the side and she seemed to be looking right through the closet door. Right at me." He raked his free hand through his hair. "And she was crying."

He was surprised to realize there was fresh moisture on his own cheeks, but he made no move to wipe it away. He must have been quiet for a long time because Candra prompted him, "You must have been terrified."

He considered that, then slowly shook his head. "No. I mean…I was scared, sure, but that's not the emotion that sticks in my mind. I was angry more than anything else. Angry at him for doing that to her and for making her cry."

"And you were angry at her."

Her words startled him so badly he jerked his hand away from her touch. "What? What are you talking about?"

"It's very common for—"

"No." He stood, walked to the bar and poured himself another brandy. He willed his hands to stop shaking. "That's ridiculous. I wasn't angry at her." He took a sip and savored the heat.

"All right." She said the words but he knew she didn't believe them. "Go on."

Because he had some strange need to be close to her he carried his snifter over to the couch and sat down again. "And then he pulled a knife."

"Oh. God."

"I wanted to get out then. I wanted to burst out of that closet and hit him and kick him. I wanted to hurt him so bad, but I didn't. I had promised her I'd stay so I did. I just kept watching her face, trying to let her know I loved her, and that she wasn't alone. And I tried…" Silently he finished, *tried to feel her pain.* He'd thought that if he could feel it, too, if she could share it with him somehow, that maybe it wouldn't hurt so much. Maybe she'd be able to hang on a little longer.

He hadn't succeeded. He hadn't been able to feel her pain, but he'd stared into her eyes, held onto her with his mind and he hadn't let go. Not until the end.

"I was only vaguely aware of what he was doing, of the blood and the motion of the knife. It was like I had tunnel vision, and could see only her face. I watched until I knew she was dead." He'd known the moment she died, had seen the light go out in her eyes and in that moment had felt the connection he sought. He'd felt a twinge, like a little tug on his soul, as if her soul had brushed against his as it fled her body. And then a deep twisting pain. "And that's the last thing I remember."

"But he didn't find you."

"No. I guess not, anyway. I don't remember. The next thing I remember is waking up one morning in a foster home. It felt like minutes later, but I guess it was actually closer to a week. I have no idea what happened in that time."

He stared into near space, waiting for the inevitable questions, the meaningless words of sympathy. But they never came.

After what might have been a moment or an hour she said only, "You're tired, Race. Why don't you lie down." He was startled to realize that she was right. He felt empty, drained, sucked dry of energy. He looked down to find that Candra had lifted the empty snifter from his grasp, and then he felt her tug on his hand. She shifted away on the couch and motioned for him to lie down, rest his head in her lap.

He blinked, tried to clear his vision that had suddenly gone fuzzy with fatigue. He wanted to lie down, to place his head just there and feel her stroke his hair, and that thought startled him. He didn't want to accept comfort, didn't deserve it, but he was too tired to fight her, too used up to protest.

He nodded and gave himself over to exhaustion, sank into her. He lay down, placed his head on her lap and let himself drift on her touch.

"I'm glad you told me, Race. It's important for you to talk about it. To share it with someone." She stroked his hair, touched his cheek. "And now that I know the whole story maybe I can help you deal with it all. Maybe you can get past it."

But she didn't know the whole story, he thought even as he drifted toward unconscious bliss. What he'd told her was only the beginning.

Chapter Seven

∾

The first few rays of watery morning sunshine drizzled through the windows and touched the back of Candra's neck. She blinked and rubbed sleep from her eyes. Not that she'd slept, really. But she had dozed on and off and had been able to find an occasional moment of rest in between dreams of flashing blades and crying children. The rest had been inadequate but, she supposed, it would have to be enough.

She looked down at Race, head still pillowed in her lap, and her lips curved. How could someone who had gone through so much, who could slice through you with his eyes and who bore the weight of so many painful memories, possibly look so innocent? Cliché or not, he looked like a little boy. With his tousled blond hair and spattering of freckles, with his eyes closed and those long lashes brushing his cheeks, he more closely resembled the innocent nine-year-old boy he'd once been, than the tortured soul she'd come to know.

With a sigh of regret, Candra eased herself out from beneath his head and replaced her lap with a suede cushion. He'd barely moved all night, sleeping so deeply and so completely that there were times when she lifted her head and gave in to the urge to check to make sure he was breathing. She would have liked to think he slept so deeply because he'd finally found some modicum of peace, but she knew it couldn't be that easy. It was a sleep born of profound exhaustion, nothing more.

Uncertain as to how much time she still had before he woke, she quickly strode from the room and made her way down the hall to the kitchen. She thought she might busy herself with making an elaborate breakfast, but first she had something else she needed to do.

She picked up the phone that hung on the wall by the stove and dialed a familiar number.

It took five rings for him to pick up.

"Holy fucking Jesus," growled a sleepy voice, "who the hell is this?"

Candra laughed. "It's me, Drew, you old grouch. And it's time to rise and shine. It's long past time for you to get up and start saving the world." She sniffed. "By the way, when *are* you going to introduce me to Spiderman. Those tights are a real turn-on."

His chuckle was low and throaty. "Ah, Candra. I'm no superhero. No matter what you like to think, I'm just a crusty old cop with a bum knee and a penchant for pizza with extra cheese."

"And catching bad guys. Don't forget that part."

"I don't catch that many. Leastways I don't catch enough."

"Hmm." Candra tapped a finger on the countertop. "By my last count you've had a hand in solving more than a dozen murders in the last four years."

"It's still not enough," he insisted.

"Well," she laughed, "you were right about one thing. You sure are crusty."

"Old, too."

"No. You're the youngest thirty-seven–year-old I know."

"I turned forty last week."

"You did not."

He laughed again. "So, is this just a social call? Because if it is, then I should really cut it short, get up and start living up to your image of me."

"See, there you go. Being a superhero isn't so hard. It's all a matter of attitude."

"Candra…" His voice held a note of warning. "What's this about? You never make this much small talk unless you're nervous about something."

"Really? I never noticed that. As a matter of fact—"

"What is it? Out with it."

She blew out a long, slow breath and resigned herself to the inevitable. "I need to ask you a favor, and I'm not sure how you'll feel about it."

"If I tackle you and lock you in a full Nelson you'll have some indication of how I feel. Or I could just say no. Now spill it."

She glanced at the doorway to the kitchen to assure herself she was still alone. "It's regarding an old murder case. I don't think it was ever solved, but frankly I can't be sure."

"You want me to look into whether the killer was caught?"

"Well, yes. I wouldn't mind knowing that, but that's pretty much a matter of public record, and honestly the information I'm looking for won't be."

He was silent, but only for a moment. "Tell me."

Very briefly she filled him in on what she knew of Race's mother's murder, then added, "He has no memory of what happened in the moments after she died, or the week after for that matter. And I'm wondering if there might be police records that could fill in some of those holes. Things like, who found him? What condition was he in? How did he cope with the investigation and being placed with a new family? Anything at all would be helpful."

"Hmm." She heard a noise, like a pen being tapped rapidly against wood. "I don't know. It would be easier if he asked himself."

"I don't think he'd do that, and I don't think I can get his permission. He's going to balk at digging up anything that opens old wounds. But I think it's essential for his treatment for me to know more about what I'm dealing with. And eventually, for him to know, as well."

Drew's finger tapped the phone. In the silence of the kitchen she gradually became aware of the chirping of birds, the soft coo of a mourning dove. The sounds drifting in through an open window signified the beginning of a brand-new day. An eternal symbol of hope.

"This isn't like you, Candra. Because of the scope of your practice, you've always been so worried about your reputation. I've never known you to…step outside the box like this. So, why now? Why take the risk?"

She smoothed a hand across the cool, marble countertop, allowed her gaze to roam over the gleaming copper pots that hung over the central island. Stainless steel appliances lined one wall, and a flat-screen computer had been tucked away in the corner. Marble and copper, oak and steel, tradition and warmth mingled with modern technology and functionality in a tentative balance. Balance. A state that was so important in life, and yet so elusive. Never more so than in the days since she'd met Race Kendall.

"Because Race is special. It's becoming personal, Drew, and I don't know what to do about it. I just know I have to do whatever it takes to help him."

"Jesus. I don't think—"

"Need I remind you about Amanda?"

The silence was so charged it made the little hairs on the back of her neck stand on end.

"Need I remind *you* how that turned out, Candra? Need I remind you how hard it was for me to pick up the pieces and keep going afterwards?"

Amanda had witnessed a brutal gangland murder. She'd clung to Drew like a bird seeking shelter from a storm, and against his better judgment he'd fallen for her—fallen for her delicate grace, sweet smile, and razor-sharp intellect. She'd vowed to help him put the killers away and he'd made it his personal mandate to protect her from those who wanted her silenced. He'd left her at his house—a place he was certain was safe—one morning just to slip out to buy milk. He'd come home to find her body hanging in his shower.

"I know it hurts," she said when she had enough control to speak, "but you wouldn't trade your time with her for anything, would you? And you wouldn't have done anything any differently."

"I wouldn't have gone to the fucking store for milk," he raged.

"Maybe. But you'd still fall in love with her."

"Yeah. I guess." The anger had already drained from his voice. "You couldn't have kept me away from her with guard dogs and razor wire. And you still couldn't."

"That's how I feel about Race. Or…at least I think I do. At this point I just know I have to try to help him. Can you help me do that?"

His sigh was answer enough.

"Thanks, Drew. Whenever you can get back to me will be fine."

She was just about to hang up when he said quietly, "By the way, Candra. Uh…"

Intrigued, Candra waited. In the ten years she'd known Drew, she'd never known him to be at a loss for words. "Yes?"

"How's Megan?"

She smiled. Drew had met Megan at a birthday party almost a year ago, and asked about her frequently. "She's fine. You should call her sometime."

"Isn't she with that…guy?"

"Eric? She still works for him, if that's what you mean."

"Yeah, right. *Works* for him."

"There's nothing else between them. At least not yet."

"He's no good for her. And I don't understand why you hang around him either."

"Eric is…complicated. You should give him a chance. You should—"

"Damn. There goes my pager. Gotta go, Candy-bar. I'll call you as soon as I have anything."

Shaking her head, she slowly hung up the phone. What was it about a beautiful woman that turned men into jealous idiots? Then she glanced down the hall and remembered how Race had looked, sleeping so soundly with the sun glowing on his cheeks, and she decided women weren't exactly immune to the idiocy factor after all.

She opened a cupboard and started looking for flour. Surely pancakes couldn't be that complicated.

Could they?

* * * * *

Race stirred. His eyelids still too heavy to force open, he sniffed the air and detected the enticing aroma of coffee and—he smiled. His mother always burned breakfast. She always had so much to do in the mornings she couldn't keep track of the eggs or the toast and—

His eyes flew open and he remembered.

He wasn't at home, hadn't been for years. He used to wake up disoriented like this, but that had been ages ago, when he was a teenager. It hadn't happened in years, and he wondered why it was happening now.

Then he sat up and took a good look at his surroundings. Gradually, through the haze of sleep and fatigue, he remembered where he was, and then he remembered how he had come to be here.

He raked his fingers through his hair and remembered the events of the night before. Pointless. The whole exercise had been so pointless. It had gotten him nothing beyond a good stiff orgasm and a fresh case of the guilts.

But then he thought of Candra and felt an odd surge of warmth.

She had fulfilled his fantasies and listened to things he hadn't told anyone—ever. She had stroked and soothed and, to his amazement, it had felt good. It had felt right. Her presence had touched something deep inside him that hadn't been touched in a very long time. Maybe it had gotten him something after all.

Dammit! He surged up off the couch and put a hand to his head as the world wavered.

It had gotten him in *trouble* was what it had gotten him. He had no right to think of her as anything other than what she was—a therapist. She was doing a job and she was doing a favor for Eric and Megan—and nothing more. Seeing her in anything other than a professional capacity was stupid, reckless and just asking for heartache.

He didn't know if his heart could take another beating. Not now. Not ever.

Focusing instead on the hollow feeling in his gut and the ache in his skull, he trudged through the house following the scent of food. Or whatever experiment she was concocting.

He stopped in the doorway, and despite the pounding inside his skull, couldn't stifle his chuckle.

She whirled on him, a spatula in one hand and a wooden spoon in the other, both dripping copious amounts of batter onto the floor. Smoke swirled around her like an ominous fog, and flour and batter spattered her robe and face. Quite a large dollop of the stuff clung to one cheek.

"What?" she demanded, her exasperation evident. "What the hell are you laughing at?"

He licked his lips and cleared his throat, but still found that he was unable to wipe the smirk off his face. "Nothing." He headed across the room to the coffeemaker. "Is the coffee ready?"

"Yes," she grumbled and then turned back to the skillet that had just sent up a fresh spurt of smoke. "The coffee is ready. *That* I know for sure. But..." she pointed a dripping spatula at the pan, "...how do you know when these things are done? How do you know when to flip them?"

He poured himself a cup of coffee and sauntered lazily over to join her. "Uh...if they're smoking, that generally means they're done."

"Smartass." She flipped one off the skillet and onto a plate, and then another, gradually building up a stack of charred disks. She shoved the plate in his direction. "Here. Enjoy."

He gave her a hooded look. "What? No bacon?"

"Don't toy with me," she growled. "I'm having a very bad day."

He laughed.

She glared.

He set down his mug and laughed until his sides ached.

At last he got enough control to suck in a deep breath and speak. "I take it you don't cook."

"I normally do frozen waffles and amazing coffee. All this sweat and toil…" she motioned grandly toward the carnage, "…represents a great sacrifice on my part."

"You used a prepackaged mix, didn't you?"

Her mutinous glare was all the answer he needed. "You have no idea how much of a challenge this was for me. You should appreciate it."

"I'll appreciate it more when my belly is full." He stuck out his hand.

She stared at it. "What?"

"Give me the spatula. I'm taking over."

"You cook?"

He bobbed his eyebrows, noticing to his amazement that his headache had disappeared. "I don't just cook. I *create*."

"Uh-huh."

He wiggled his fingers. "Come on. Hand it over."

"Do I have to help?"

"No. Please don't. Just keep the coffee coming."

She slapped the spatula into his palm. "It is good, isn't it? The coffee, I mean."

"Best I've had all day."

"Smartass."

"Now get out of my way. I wouldn't want you to get hurt."

Laughing in spite of herself, she poured herself a huge mug of java and pulled up a stool to watch. He felt a little like he was on stage but strangely he didn't mind. Strangely, he kind of liked it.

He dumped out what remained of the batter in the bowl, pitched the bag of pancake mix and grabbed the flour. He hoped he remembered. It had been a very long time.

Candra sat on her stool, sipped from her coffee and watched him work. His movements were efficient, economical, his concentration intense. He was so focused on his task and yet his expression had lost the iciness — the sense of isolation — of previous encounters. She could swear, every once in a while, she could still see a hint of a smile twitching at the corners of his mouth.

There. He'd just done it again.

"You're still laughing at my expense," she said. "Aren't you?"

He picked up a cup of fresh blueberries that he had somehow managed to produce out of the enormous refrigerator, and dumped them into the batter. He folded them in with long, smooth strokes.

"You didn't answer me."

He poured a dollop of the batter into the skillet and was rewarded with a satisfying sizzle. Bacon, already fried to a crisp, golden brown had been set in the oven to keep warm. He shrugged, but she could tell he was working hard to suppress a grin.

She slipped off the stool and sidled up to him. "You were surprised because I'm a woman and I can't cook, is that it? I should be genetically predisposed to knowing how to handle a whisk."

"No." He watched his creations as they sizzled and bubbled. "I was surprised because you seem like such a capable, in-control person. I just assumed you'd know how to handle yourself in the kitchen —" he sliced her a look, " — as well as the bedroom." He flipped a pancake. "Office. Whatever."

She moved in behind him, slid her hands around his waist. She sensed his surprise, but he merely continued flipping and pouring. "I maintain that if I were a man, you wouldn't have found it so amusing." She reached for the knot on his robe and began to loosen it.

"*I* maintain that I would have laughed at someone who had batter all over their face, regardless of sex."

Her hands stopped. "Batter on their face?" She reached up, found a large damp spot on her cheek and quickly wiped it away. She swatted the back of his head. "You jerk. You didn't tell me."

"You didn't ask."

She grabbed his belt and whirled him to face her. His eyes were laughing at her. Damn, it was good to see.

"Hey," he protested. "I've still got some cooking to do."

The knot came undone and the lapels fell open. She stroked his penis and was pleased to see it rise to her touch. "Ain't that the truth."

"I really need to keep an eye on the pancakes."

She reached up and slipped the robe from his shoulder. "You just go right ahead and do whatever it is…" she waved toward the skillet, "…you do. I'll just sit back and watch."

The robe slid down, held in place at his wrists by the utensils he clutched in his hands. "You want me to cook naked?"

"Is there any other way?"

"Hmm." But he must have seen the merit in her suggestion because he shifted the spatula from one hand to the other, allowing the robe to fall to the floor. He turned back to the skillet. "These are almost done. Could you get a plate?"

"Sure," she purred, whisking her fingers across the curve of his ass on her way to the cupboard. Keeping her gaze half on him and enjoying the erotic little movements and twitches of the muscles in his back and arms, she pulled out a couple of Limoges plates. She had barely set the plates on the counter beside him before he flipped a set of four perfectly round, perfectly golden flapjacks off the griddle.

He picked up the bottle of maple syrup and proceeded to drizzle it over the pancakes.

She raked her eyes over the lines of his body, the angles of his jaw, down the sinewy length of his arms, and finally dropped her gaze to the plate. She recalled the way his body had slipped through the water as he swam and the sweet tones he had coaxed out of that piano and shook her head in amazement. "Is there anything you can't do, Mr. Kendall? Anything at all?"

He said nothing and when she lifted her gaze to his she was shocked to see that the pain in his eyes was back. When he spoke she knew why.

"I can't bring my mother back," he whispered. "Can I?"

"Race." Instinctively she reached for him. She grasped his wrist and was relieved when he didn't pull away. "It wasn't your fault. I know it's not enough to hear it, but it's all I've got."

Suddenly he wrapped his arms around her and drew her in tight. "No," he breathed. "No, it's not all you've got." And then he sealed his mouth to hers.

The kiss was fierce, hungry, as if he were searching for something. She couldn't give him the thing he sought the most, but she could give him something else — herself. She melted into the kiss, this time holding nothing back. She allowed all the walls to crumble, all her will to dissolve, and granted him access to the deepest parts of her. Her robe remained in place but in the truest sense of the words, she felt naked and completely vulnerable.

His grip on her still like iron, his mouth separated from hers and he began peppering kisses down her throat. "Jesus," he breathed. "What was that?"

Her eyes closed as he pushed the robe off one shoulder and nibbled on her collarbone. "I thought it was a kiss."

"That was no kiss." He lifted his head and she opened her eyes to find him gazing down at her. "That was an apocalypse."

She licked her lips, suddenly a little unsure of herself and what she was doing—and not sure why. His gaze was as intense as his kiss, and just as unnerving.

"Wh-what about breakfast?" Her hands cruised around his waist and up his back. She flicked her tongue at his nipple.

"Does that mean you're hungry?"

She arched her eyebrows. "You know I am."

She expected him to lead her out of the kitchen or, perhaps, to hoist her up onto the counter and ravish her right there, but he did neither. Instead, he reached for a pancake and tore off a hunk. He lifted the piece, dripping with syrup and blueberry juice, and set it against her lips.

"Then eat."

Her heart felt like a hammer inside her chest as she licked tentatively at the morsel with her tongue. He held it still, allowing her to nibble and then to draw it into her mouth as she saw fit. When she'd swallowed the last of it, she drew his fingers into her mouth and suckled them lightly. "Mmm," she groaned. "A delicacy."

Desire smoldering in his eyes, he asked, "More?"

"Please."

He reached for another piece, only this time he placed it between his own lips—and smiled.

"You want me to work for it this time?"

He nodded.

She reached up, wrapped a hand around the back of his neck and drew him down to her. She nibbled at the pancake, tentatively at first, allowing the excess syrup to drizzle from the corners of her mouth and down her chin. She continued nibbling, lapping up syrup with her tongue and working her way toward him until at last their lips met and their mouths melded. They kissed deeply, sharing the sweetness and the passion until nothing remained in their mouths but heat.

She drew away and allowed him to lick at the syrup that still clung to her chin as she skimmed her hands down his chest and sought his cock. She found it hard and stroked the damp tip with her thumb.

And then she grinned. "I bet that would taste great with syrup, too."

"You read my mind," he murmured, his mouth against her throat. And then, abruptly he shifted away, pushed the robe from her shoulders and slid her thong down her thighs. "Almost," he said with a grin as he lifted her by the waist and set her on the counter. He pushed her knees apart and stepped between them.

"What the—"

His thumb on her clit sent a little bolt of electricity through her and ceased all verbal protests. He massaged her, keeping her occupied as he reached for the syrup. She watched in wonder as he finally withdrew his hand, drizzled the confection over her pussy and then bent to taste her.

She had to grip the edge of the counter to keep from toppling off as his tongue cruised over her sex, suckled her clit and then dipped inside her. She squirmed and he grasped her hips to hold her as he continued, uttering soft groans of delight as he sought out and lapped up every last drop of syrup, every last bead of her own moisture.

She muttered his name, uncertain what she was asking for, but when he stood and faced her, his cock nudging her pussy, she knew. He thrust inside her and she wrapped her legs around him, accepting him deep and, for just that moment, forgetting herself. She wanted to feel him, feel all of him against her flesh. "My bra," she pleaded, reaching for the clasp at the back. "Please."

"No." He grasped her wrists and guided them to his shoulders. She felt a tension there, a bunching of the muscles that had nothing to do with his arousal. "Leave it." He thrust again, deeper this time. Harder. "It's a turn-on."

Even as his thrusts quickened and his mouth sought hers for a deep kiss that tasted of syrup and sex, she remembered. She remembered where she was and what she was supposed to be doing. As he plunged himself into her and she gripped his back to keep from falling, she reminded herself that it couldn't be that easy. A spontaneous fuck on the kitchen counter didn't mean anything had changed. Race Kendall still had a long way to go.

A climax built in her center and she sealed her mouth to his, accepting his tongue and drawing in his cock so deep that it nudged her womb. The orgasm crashed over her and pounded through her. He groaned in his own release, his climax no doubt just as powerful as her own.

And yet, when he pulled away and smiled at her, she sensed the distance in his gaze. The residual tension that her request had left in his shoulders.

He turned toward the oven. "So, how about some bacon with that? Somehow I'm hungrier now than I was before." He grinned at her. "Go figure."

"Sure. Anything you put in my mouth I'll eat." She said it with a smile and a lift of an eyebrow, but in her heart she knew—nothing had changed. Despite the light mood and the intense climax, there had been no sharing in that kitchen. It had been a moment of physical and sexual release, and nothing more.

Somehow she had to break through that shell and touch what lay beneath. She was running out of ideas, however, and hoped that whatever answers Drew came up with would help her find the hairline crack that would shatter Race's defenses and allow her inside to touch the thing that most needed touching. His soul.

Chapter Eight

හ

Candra closed her office door, leaned back against it and rubbed her forehead.

"Some therapist I am," she muttered to herself. Poor Donald was paying her good money to help him overcome his impotence, and all she could think about was the way Race had looked when she left him at Eric's.

He'd been standing beside the pool, gloriously nude and gleaming in the midmorning sun as he prepared to dive in for his ritual fifty laps. He'd looked alone and just a little sad and she couldn't quite put her finger on why. She'd wanted to kiss him goodbye, but realized that was the kind of thing a couple indulged in, and she had to keep reminding herself that they *weren't* a couple, or at least that they weren't supposed to be. She'd managed to stifle the urge and had parted with a friendly wave and a promise to be back early for the supper that he was "creating" for her that evening.

Couple or not he was cooking for her. Again.

She knew full well that she'd already nudged a toe over the line, but knowing it and admitting it to herself and, of course, to *Race* were two completely different matters. She continued to hide behind the illusion that this was all about Race's sexual and emotional health and that since he'd agreed to an intensive therapy session after dinner—one that involved her sitting on one side of the table, and him sitting opposite her—that somehow validated the event.

She headed back to her desk, sat down and made a note on her day planner to give Donald a discount on his next visit. Thank God she'd only had two clients booked for that afternoon. It had been hard enough to leave Race for a few hours—a whole day would have been intolerable.

She dropped her forehead onto the blotter littered with paperclips, curlicues and cryptic notes, and groaned. How had it gotten this bad? How had she let herself start caring so much? This couldn't be healthy for either of them. But was that going to stop her?

No way.

A knock on the door startled her.

"Candra?" called a woman from the outer office. "Are you in there?"

Candra lifted her head. "Megan? Yeah, I'm here."

The door opened and Megan stepped inside. Smiling and looking classy and casual in champagne-colored silk and stone-washed jeans, she crossed to the desk—and frowned.

Candra blinked. "What?"

Megan reached out and plucked something off Candra's forehead. She held up her prize. "Are you leaking paperclips from your brain again? I thought you got that little problem looked after."

Candra chuckled, then looked at Megan and hesitated. "Oh no. We were supposed to go out for supper tonight, weren't we? We were going to check out that new Steven Woo movie."

Megan nodded.

Candra leaned back in her chair, closed her eyes and pressed a palm to her forehead. "You know, I may not have paperclips in my brain, but I don't seem to have much else lately."

"Oh, I don't know about that," said Megan, hitching a hip onto the edge of the desk. "You've got something in there, all right, and its name is Race."

Candra cracked open an eye.

"You have plans with him don't you?"

"Uh…yeah. A session. Over at Eric's."

"Uh-huh."

"And he's cooking for me."

Megan nodded. "I figured as much."

"But how—"

"I talked to Eric this afternoon and he had just talked to Race." She grinned. "Plus I know that Race is dynamite in the kitchen and I knew you'd never be able to resist that."

"Shoot, Meg. I'm sorry I forgot, but I just don't know what's gotten into me. Ever since meeting Race I'm hopelessly distracted. I'm useless here, I'm jeopardizing my practice and I'm not even sure how much good I'm doing him."

"Trust me, you're good for him, and you're not jeopardizing anything." Megan slipped off the desk. "Except maybe your heart. I don't mind giving up a dinner date with you if it means you've finally found a man to care about."

Candra stiffened. "What are you talking about? I've had plenty of boyfriends. It's not my fault that they all kept worrying that I was evaluating their sexual techniques and diagnosing their psychoses."

"That's an excuse. None of them were right for you, Candra, and you know it. None of them were strong enough." She leaned in closer. "You needed more of a challenge, and Race is nothing if not a challenge."

Candra opened her mouth to retort, but then slowly closed it again. Maybe Megan was right. Sometimes things were so much clearer when seen from the other side of the fence. Maybe a different perspective was exactly what she needed—what they both needed.

She slapped her hands on her knees. "Okay, that's it. You're coming to dinner."

Megan's eyebrows arched. "I'm what?"

"You heard me." She stood. "I intend to make up for forgetting about our evening by having Race cook for you."

"I don't know."

"Don't even think about arguing." She grabbed Megan's arm and steered her toward the door. "I won't take no for an answer, so you just—"

The trill of her office phone interrupted her. She glared at it, considered not answering and then caught a glimpse of the number in the caller ID box. She snatched up the receiver. "Hi, Drew. What did you find out?"

He let out a soft snort. "Well, I'm just fine. Thanks for asking. What would your mother say if she knew how you treated me?"

"She'd laugh in your face and say you wouldn't know good manners if they reared up and bit you in the ass."

He chuckled. "I know. That's exactly what she'd say."

She glanced at Megan who had moved over to the window to give her some privacy, but Candra had noticed the way her eyes glinted at the mention of Drew's name.

"So? Don't keep me in suspense. You found something out or else you wouldn't have called me."

"Yeah. I did." The subtle but unmistakable shift in his tone made the hairs on the back of her neck stand up.

"Is it bad?"

Megan turned to look at her, her face a question mark.

Candra shrugged.

"Bad enough that I'm having second thoughts about telling you," said Drew.

"If it's that bad then that's all the more reason to tell me. For Race's sake, Drew. Please."

She heard his sigh and knew she'd won. "Okay, but you owe me for this one, Candra. You owe me big."

She picked up a pen and a pad of paper. "I'll save your life someday and we'll call it even, okay? Now tell me."

* * * * *

Race sliced the last mushroom and dropped it into the pot. The enormous stockpot was full to bursting with tomatoes, beef, beans, chilies and a few ingredients that he'd now be hard-pressed to name. He'd made enough to feed a small platoon of ration-starved GIs, but chili just didn't work out right if you thought small.

He dipped the wooden spoon into the bubbling concoction and lifted it to his lips for a taste. He nodded approval, and then he grinned.

No doubt Candra was expecting a gourmet meal of chicken and pesto, or perhaps cedar-plank salmon. When he'd plied her with tales of his culinary accomplishments, telling her of the year spent in the home of a woman who had studied under Julia Child, she'd of course made the automatic assumption. He hadn't bothered to tell her that he had no taste for five-star restaurants or shrimp and mango chutney on a bed of wild rice and radicchio. He shuddered at the thought.

His tastes ran to thick steaks, barbecued ribs and chili that could put hair on the chest of a fourteen-year-old virgin. He tested the brew again. "Mmm," he murmured to himself, as the tears welled in his eyes. "Perfect."

He glanced at the clock, wondering if Candra's appointments had concluded on time. Of course the chili would be good for hours—days even—but he was anxious to see her reaction, to see the surprise on her face and the glint of humor in her eyes.

It had been a long time since he'd enjoyed seeing someone smile that much, and that thought scared him spitless. He turned from the stove and walked to the window where he could see the burgeoning colors of a Pacific sunset.

It was tough to admit, but it had been a long time since he'd been this eager to see someone, since he'd cared this much. But the trouble was, he wasn't sure if it was because of who she was or *what* she was. Was it the woman in her that was inspiring these first tiny buds of trust and, yes, hope? Or was it the therapist who was digging deeply and touching places that had remained untouched since childhood? And if so, what happened when her job was done? Where did that leave them?

Where did that leave him?

And then he turned away from the window and laughed, but even to his own ears the sound was hollow, echoing against the hard, cold kitchen surfaces. To think of her job being "done" implied that he could eventually be cured of the emotional burdens that weighed on him, that his ghosts could be exorcised. And that was impossible because that would mean sharing everything with her, and no one knew — had ever known — the full extent of his secrets. Not that she'd believe him anyway. More than likely she'd call the men in the white coats to come and take him away.

How could she possibly believe him when some days he wondered himself if he was hallucinating everything?

But as he headed for the cupboard and reached for the plates to finish setting the table, he knew he wasn't hallucinating the pain that stabbed through his side or the pressure across his throat. And he knew he wasn't imagining the crash of the dishes or the sting as shards of broken china pierced his bare feet as he staggered forward.

Doubled over in pain and lost in a world of terror, scratching branches and rocks that dug into his source's back and scalp, he accepted the truth and accepted the fact that nothing could change this. Nothing could change where he'd come from or what he'd become.

Short of death, nothing—and no one—could release him from this hell that was his life.

* * * * *

"Race?" called Candra, her voice echoing through the cavernous entryway. "I brought company!"

"Is that a warning to make sure he's decent?" asked Megan.

"It's a warning to make sure he has some clothes on. I don't delude myself into thinking Race is anything close to decent."

Megan chuckled as Candra continued to lead her through the house, following the enticing aromas of garlic and spices. "Race?" she tried again, surprised that he hadn't come up with a suitably scathing response to her little surprise. "Did you hear me?"

"Maybe he's outside," offered Megan as they neared the kitchen. "Or playing the piano."

"Maybe. But it seems like an odd time to choose to do that."

They stepped into the kitchen and, as expected, found it empty. An enormous pot sat on the stove and a pair of candles adorned the large pine table. Glasses and cutlery had been set out, but not yet arranged. "He said he hates the dining room," said Candra, by way of explanation. "He finds it depressing."

"Oh." Megan crossed to the stove and peeked into the pot. "Chili." She sniffed. "Mmm. It smells wonderful."

"Chili?" Candra rounded the island and looked for herself. "He made me *chili*?"

"What?" asked Megan. "You were expecting, maybe, sushi?"

"No, but—" And then she noticed the floor. "Oh my God!"

"What?" Megan rounded the counter and stopped. "What the hell? Is that blood?"

Candra was already kneeling beside the carnage. She touched a red droplet and her finger came away wet. "It's fresh. Must have happened just before we got here." She pointed to a series of bloody impressions. "Footprints. He's gone already. The bastard took off without even leaving a note."

"Happened? What happened? What are you talking about?"

"I'm pretty sure he had another episode."

"Episode? You mean like at the party? But what does that mean?"

Candra stood and faced her friend. "Come with me and I'll explain on the way."

"On the way where?" wailed Megan.

"To Race's. For once in his life he has someone who cares enough to not let him get away with this shit. We're going to find him and find out what the hell he's doing, and we're going to help him no matter what obstacles he throws in our way."

"B-but if he doesn't want to be found shouldn't we respect his wishes?"

"You're kidding, right?" said Candra as they headed out the side door. "Surely you know me better than that."

Megan chuckled. "Yeah. I guess I do."

Chapter Nine

❧

Race raked his fingers through his hair and stared, bleary-eyed, at the computer screen. He'd been at it for almost twenty-three hours now, yet was no closer to determining who the victim was or where the attack had taken place than he had been yesterday. He was running out of time and urgency made him desperate.

And desperation made him sloppy.

Once again his connection to the victim had been intense, but in this case it had been all too brief. The attack, quick and brutal, had lasted less than five minutes from start to finish, and the victim's vision had been obscured for most of that time. He had a name, but all leads with regard to tracing her whereabouts had come up empty. Likely she was a street hooker without an address or a traceable past. Of course that had happened before, but he'd almost always had a good idea as to the location of the attack and had been able to intercept the events there. Not so this time.

All he had were a few brief impressions that included trees and rocks, the distant sound of surf and one fleeting glimpse of a wrought iron fence topped with intricate finials shaped like tulips. The trouble was there were dozens of parks along the coast, and despite his frantic search, he'd been unable to find one that boasted that particular kind of wrought iron fencing. And yet…there was something familiar about it, as if he'd seen it before. As if he *should* know exactly where this place was, and the inability to remember was making him crazy.

He glanced at his watch. Forty minutes. "Dammit, Tawnya," he murmured, eyes closed, mind focused. "I'm sorry. But I just don't know what else—"

His eyes flew open and in that instant he *knew*. "Shit," he shouted. "Shit, shit, *shit*!" It wasn't a park at all. It was a fucking graveyard and he knew exactly where it was. The thing was it was a good forty-five-minute drive away, and that left him no time to prepare, let alone get there. He grabbed his bag and dashed out the door, swearing to himself that he would get there.

No matter what, he'd get there in time.

* * * * *

Megan took a sip of coffee and cringed as the tepid brew swirled over her tongue. It had been sitting in the cup holder too long. She glanced at her watch. Almost as long as she'd been sitting in this damn car. She glanced at the slumbering figure of Candra in the driver's seat next to her. She'd been up almost all night, leaving her exhausted, her yawns so huge Megan could feel the suction from the other side of the car. It had become ridiculous and Megan had insisted that Candra put her seat back and catch a few winks while Megan continued the "stakeout" on her own.

She looked out the window at the apartment that was the focus of their little surveillance session, and grinned. Who'd have thought she, Megan Chambers, would ever be involved in something so...devious? Not that she could take much credit. It had all been Candra's doing—persistent, tenacious, meticulous, unrelenting Candra.

When a visit to Race's house—which included picking his locks and risking a breaking and entering charge—had yielded nothing, Candra had turned to her friend Drew. Megan smiled at the thought of the crusty cop with the soft brown eyes.

Drew had refused to put out an APB on Race, but had obliged them by checking to see if Race had any other properties or leases where he might be holed up. When that search had come up empty, Candra had asked Drew to check under Race's birth name which, for some reason, he'd abandoned at the age of eighteen in favor of the name Kendall.

She'd hit the jackpot. Race Malone did indeed have a small apartment rented in the east end of the city, and Candra and Megan had immediately driven to the address. The curtains were all pulled so they couldn't see inside, but they were sure he was there since the pickup truck which was also registered under the name Race Malone was clearly visible in the apartment's carport.

Candra had parked the car, but had made no move to get out, and when prompted by Megan, had said that she thought maybe they shouldn't go in. She doubted he would answer the door anyway, and she didn't think breaking into the third-floor apartment was a good idea. Maybe they should just watch for a while and see what happened. He had to come out sometime, and she wanted to know where he went, and what he was up to, when he did.

That had been four hours ago. And now they waited.

Megan was focused on the apartment, her eyes growing heavy and she was just considering waking Candra and taking her own turn at catching a few "z"s, when Candra's cell phone chirped.

Candra jolted awake as if she'd heard a fire alarm rather than a cheerful rendition of "The Entertainer". She snatched up the phone and clicked it on. "Hello?" She raked her fingers through her hair. "Oh. Hi, Drew. What's up?"

Curious, Megan watched Candra, anticipating a reaction. She wasn't disappointed. A moment later Candra's face registered surprise, and then outright concern. "You're kidding," she breathed. "But why would he need a gun?"

Megan blinked, fighting her own shock.

"Don't be ridiculous, Drew," continued Candra. And then, "Of course. Of course I will." She rolled her eyes and cast an impatient glance at Megan. "Yes, Drew. I promise."

A moment later she clicked off and turned a wide-eyed gaze on Megan. "Race owns a gun. A handgun."

"Yes. I heard."

"And Drew wants me to call him the second Race shows his face, or anything happens."

"He thinks Race is a threat?"

Candra nodded. "But that's ridiculous. I'm sure—"

The roar of an engine cut through the quiet evening air, and both women riveted their gaze on the carport.

"Shit," said Candra, turning the key in the ignition, "I didn't see him come out."

A moment later he screamed out of the driveway, building up so much speed as he rounded the corner that he fishtailed, leaving a long black strip of rubber in his wake.

"Damn it!" Candra peeled off after him. "I hope I can keep up." She tossed the phone to Megan. "Call Drew back for me. If I don't keep my promise he'll never forgive me."

"Yeah," chuckled Megan. "He's almost as stubborn as you are."

Candra growled an unintelligible retort, but kept her eyes on the road and the pair of taillights that were gradually getting smaller as the truck sped down the highway into the distance.

* * * * *

Race screamed to a stop in the small parking lot at the bottom of the hill. With a quick glance at the hillside dotted with headstones, maple trees and thick hedges, he erupted from the truck and threw his backpack to the ground. Without bothering to check his watch—he already knew he was almost out of time—he rummaged through the pack in search of what he needed. He might be in a rush, but going in unprepared and unarmed would help neither him nor the victim.

Dart gun in hand, and knife strapped to his leg, he rushed through the gate and headed up the hill. The attack had happened near the top of a rise. A glimpse of a spectacular ocean view in his vision had told him that much.

The distant scream that echoed through the night confirmed it. He ran toward the source of the sound, darting around trees and bushes, and batting away branches that threatened to tear at his skin and gouge out his eyes.

He crested the hill and saw a flash of movement off to his right. Gun drawn, he dashed through a pair of hedges—and skidded to a halt. He was too late.

The wound in her throat gaped, her blood continuing to pump out, slowly soaking the grass around her head—and staining his very soul. It had slowed to a trickle, lacking the vigor of an actively beating heart but it was in her eyes that he saw death. He'd seen that flat, sightless, haunting quality before. He'd seen it once too often.

He raised the pistol and aimed at the man who was crouched over her body, cutting away her clothes and preparing to defile her in ways too heinous to imagine.

"You fucking son of a—"

The man looked up, noticing him at last, and Race realized he'd made a horrible mistake. Once again he was paralyzed, his finger stalled on the trigger and the breath caught in his chest, burning there as an irrational terror poured through him. He felt weak, boneless, had to take a step back to steady himself, and completely lacked the strength to aim and fire his weapon.

"You!" said the man, leaping from the body and turning on Race. He raised a pistol, clutching it tightly in bloodstained fingers — and aiming it at Race's chest. "Who the hell *are* you?"

"Get away from her," said Race, the words a rough whisper that tore at his throat. "You'll pay for this. I swear — "

He felt the bullet a split second before he heard the report of the shot. His body lurched backward, a white-hot pain flaring through his chest and crushing his lungs. Even as he hit the ground he knew — realized he had always known — that he would die like this, at the hands of a monster, alone and helpless. He just didn't think it would hurt quite this much.

And he never thought it would happen quite so soon.

"Stupid fuck!" Anton stepped toward the body of the man who had interfered with his plans for the last time. He didn't take more than two steps, however, before the scream of a woman halted him in his tracks.

"Race! Race, are you okay?"

And then the voice of a man. "Up there! I think it came from up there!"

"Shit!" Anton glanced at the man who lay at his feet and noted that he was still breathing. One more shot was all it would take, but he couldn't risk it. Not with a pair of witnesses scurrying up the hillside toward him. With one final, longing glance at the body of the woman that he'd been so ripe to take, he dashed for the cover of the thick hedgerow behind him on the crest of the hill.

He'd just barely rounded the bushes when he heard the crack of a twig and an exclamation of surprise. Deciding it wise to take it slow, and keep quiet, he stopped to catch his breath and take stock of what he was up against. He huddled down, and through the deep green leaves of the hedge he watched as three people came crashing onto the scene and bent over the two victims.

It was the woman however, the woman with the long mahogany-colored hair and the big blue eyes that caught his attention. She was beautiful, striking, her bearing proud and arresting even as she fell to her knees beside the man. She bent over him, touching his face with the kind of tenderness that spoke of intimacy and affection. "Race?" she said, her voice laced with fear and concern. "Race, can you hear me?"

He groaned, and Anton's worst fears were confirmed. Most likely this…*Race* would live and that could only spell disaster for Anton.

Or at least it would if Anton didn't do something to remedy the situation. And he intended to, but for now he'd have to wait.

He'd watch and plan and pick his time carefully and next time he wouldn't make any mistakes. He glanced at the woman and grinned as he slipped away into the gathering darkness.

* * * * *

Candra cradled Race's head in her lap and pressed a hand to the wound in his chest. It was well away from his heart, but he was losing a lot of blood and his breathing was weak and ragged.

Tears trickled down her cheeks and terror pooled in her gut.

"The ambulance and police are on their way," said Drew, crouching beside her, gun in one hand, cell phone in the other. "Don't worry."

She looked at him and saw a murderous rage in his eyes. "Drew. I…I'm sorry. I don't know how I could have been so wrong about him. But I never dreamed…" She couldn't bring herself to complete the thought.

He frowned. "What?" Megan knelt beside him and suddenly his face registered understanding. "Oh God, Candra. No. Race didn't do this. He didn't attack that woman."

She blinked. "He didn't?"

"No. Of course not. I did a quick search and didn't see anyone, so it looks like whoever it was got away. But the footprints around her body are far too small to belong to Race, and I have no doubt that the knife I found will yield a completely different set of prints."

Candra tried to assimilate that. She'd come upon the scene, had taken in the woman's body and just made the automatic assumption. But now, thinking about it, she realized Race couldn't possibly have done it. For one thing, he didn't have time since she and Drew had barely been a minute behind him.

"B-but what was he doing here?"

"He was trying to save her," said Megan. "I'm sure of it."

The wail of the ambulance siren calling from the distance, she looked down at the man who lay in her arms, struggling for life, and knew that Megan was right. But that raised a whole new crop of questions. Huge questions. Questions that she just hoped Race would eventually be able to answer.

She bent low and kissed his forehead. "You're gonna make it, Race. I've invested way too much in you to let you die on me now."

Chapter Ten
Six weeks later

စာ

Candra picked up a leaf of lettuce and shredded it thoughtfully into the bowl in front of her. The surface of the counter was pitted and crisscrossed with knife marks, the pine cupboard doors just as battered and used. Her parents' seaside cottage had been in the family for years and had taken the abuse of two generations' worth of progeny. Many might look at the surroundings and feel the need to renovate and renew. But for Candra every rip in the worn couch and every dent in the pine four-poster bed in the main bedroom had significance. They spoke of childhoods filled with tickle-fights and games of tag. They spoke of warmth and happiness and the kind of life someone like Race Kendall could only dream of.

Lace curtains, yellowed by years of exposure to sun and salty breezes, billowed into the room. From the kitchen window she could see the blue sparkling waters of the Pacific Ocean, she could watch seagulls wheeling overhead, and she could just make out the lonely figure of a man sitting in the sand. He hadn't moved in hours, had remained perfectly still, knees drawn up to his chest, and eyes focused on the horizon as the water gradually rose, drawing ever closer to his bare, sun-baked toes.

She sighed, set aside the bowl and picked up a towel to dry her hands. "Dammit, Race," she muttered as she replaced the towel on its hook and headed for the bedroom. "You've wallowed long enough. It's time for me to start getting tough."

Five minutes later, clad only in a red string bikini and a towel, she plopped herself down beside him in the sand.

He said nothing, didn't even turn his head to look at her.

"It's been six weeks, Race. Your physical wounds have almost completely healed. You're running out of excuses."

He took a deep breath and she caught the little wince that he tried so hard to hide from her. Although she was trying to be tough and strong, the knowledge that breathing deeply still caused him some pain, weakened her resolve. Some, but not enough.

"I'm not making excuses," he said at last. "I want to go home and go back to work. You're the one who's insisting I still need more time to heal. You're the one who insisted on bringing me here after they let me out of the hospital."

"That's not what I'm talking about and you know it. I'm not talking about going back home or starting back to work."

He turned his gaze on her, and the fact that it lacked any trace of fire or anger worried her more than his breathing or his weakened physical state.

"Then what the hell are you talking about?"

She shook her head in exasperation. "All right. If that's the way it has to be." She turned so she was facing him. "You're sullen and withdrawn, Race. You eat little and talk less and have refused to answer any of the questions I've asked you."

"I talked to the police plenty. That Drew friend of yours is a real pain in the ass."

"You're not being straight with him and he knows it."

He narrowed his eyes and opened his mouth as if to retort, and then seemed to think better of it. He closed his mouth, flexed his jaw.

"Whatever it is, Race, you can tell me. You can trust me with anything. Surely you know that."

His laughter surprised her. "You have no idea what you're talking about."

"I know that you have mysterious episodes that resemble seizures, and that every time you have one you disappear for days on end. I know you have an apartment that you keep under a pseudonym and that it's outfitted with stacks of high-tech computer and surveillance equipment, not to mention tranquilizer darts, a handgun and various other weapons. I know that you had some sort of information about that attack and knew enough about it to intercept it as it was happening." She paused for breath. "I also know all that has made the police extremely suspicious of you, and that you should come clean with them. You should tell them the truth so that they can dispense with their suspicions and get on with catching this guy."

Race's jaw was set, his eyes smoldering. "You know so much. You *know* that telling the police the truth is the right thing to do."

"Of course it is. The truth is always the right choice."

"Is it?"

She felt strangely unsettled by that little question. "Of course it is."

"How about going to prison for the rest of my life. Is *that* the right choice?"

That startled her. "What are you talking about?"

He flopped back on the sand. "See? You have no idea what you're talking about. And you wouldn't believe me, anyway."

She lay down on the sand, facing him, her head propped on her hand, the waves lapping at her feet. "You don't trust me."

Very slowly he turned toward her. "I trust you more than I've ever trusted anyone."

"But it's still not enough."

He looked at the sky. "It's the best I can do."

She lay there, considering him, and considering what she had planned to do. His "episodes" were only one symptom of the problem that needed addressing. There was another.

Very slowly she sat up, knelt beside him and sat back on her haunches, facing him. "And this is this is the best *I* can do." And then she reached for the ties that held her bikini top in place.

"What? What are you doing?" She heard the edge in his voice and knew she was doing the right thing.

The two tiny triangles of fabric fell to the sand. "Touch me, Race."

His Adam's apple bobbed. "If you're trying to seduce me, this is a helluva way to go about it."

"I'm not trying to seduce you. I just want you to touch my breasts. You've never touched them."

He sat up, but didn't reach for her. "I'm not in the mood."

She watched him, saw the way his breathing had picked up, the way the color had drained from his cheeks. It was an irrational reaction, an unrealistic fear. He was displaying the reaction of a phobic, and God knew he had good reason for it.

"You've never touched a woman's breasts, have you?"

He turned away from her, eyes closed, fists clenched.

"That's one of the things your girlfriends had a problem with, isn't it? One of the…*issues*. And I'd guess it was rather a big one."

He scrubbed his hands over his face and whispered, "I've tried. God knows I've tried, but I can't…" He shook his head, glanced at her, and then looked away. "At times it's so bad it makes me sick to my stomach, and I don't know what to do about it and I don't know why." He launched from the sand and whirled on her, his voice building as the rage leaked out. "What's wrong with me? A man who is *afraid* of a pair of beautiful breasts? Jesus fucking Christ! What kind of man am I?" He whirled around and his shoulders shook with the anger and frustration that was pent-up inside him.

Taking pity on him she replaced her bikini top and stood to approach him. She laid a hand on his forearm, and when he tried to jerk away she held on tight.

"I know why, Race. And I think it's time you did, too."

* * * * *

"Are you there, Race? Are you in your old apartment?" Candra's voice came to him as if through a fog, distant and nebulous, and yet the words and their meaning were clear. Strange, he thought, to be hypnotized, and yet be completely aware of that fact.

He knew he was in the guest room of her parent's cottage, lounging back on a mountain of pillows with Candra beside him. Physically he was there, mentally he'd traveled back in time more than twenty years.

"Yes," he said, even as he brushed a virtual fingertip across the polished keys of the piano. They were cool to the touch and he longed to play them but then he heard a sickening scream and remembered why he was there. He looked toward the bedroom—*his* old bedroom.

"You have to go into the bedroom, Race. You need to do that now."

"I don't want to." Already the fear was knotting in his gut.

"I know you don't. But you have to. It's important."

Nodding gravely, he walked toward the doorway to his old room. His feet felt like they were made of wet clay but, compelled by Candra's voice, he forced them to move. He reached the doorway and hesitated only briefly before stepping across the threshold.

His mother's attacker loomed over her bloodied body. She lay on the blood-soaked bed, stripped naked, her chest and abdomen a grisly patchwork of knife wounds and bruises.

He felt strangely calm, however, the fear that had begun to well up in him, magically disappearing, as if someone had pulled a plug and it had all drained away.

"Are you in the bedroom?" asked Candra's voice.

"Yes."

"Are you all right? Are you calm and disconnected, just like we talked about?"

That was why he was so calm, he realized, because she'd instructed him to be so. He was to remain disconnected from his memories, watch the events unfold as a dispassionate observer. At least, that was the objective. "Yes."

"Tell me what he's doing."

He swallowed hard, his emotions battering the wall Candra had constructed for him. It trembled and shook, but it held. "He's raping her."

"Is she crying? Screaming?"

"No." He blinked. "She's dead."

"So she's not feeling anything, is she? She's not there anymore."

He wanted to close his eyes but forced them to stay open because he had to. "No. She's not."

"You have to believe that. It's the truth, and it's important."

He merely nodded, assimilating that. Trying desperately to take it to heart.

His mother's killer appeared to be getting frustrated. Something wasn't right, and he was getting angry. He slapped his victim, and yelled something obscene. Her head snapped to the side, and Race's stomach twisted. But he tamped it down, distanced himself from it.

"What's happening now?" asked Candra. "Tell me what you're seeing."

Race opened his mouth to speak but then the words caught on his tongue as the killer reached into his pocket and pulled out—despite Candra's instructions, his stomach twisted and he felt sick. "He took out the knife again. It's covered in her blood. Oh God. I can't do this."

Candra kept her voice calm and even despite the fact that her heart was pounding in her throat. "Yes, you can, Race. You have to."

This was the moment, the key to everything. She hated that he had to go through this, hated watching his face go pale, the sweat break out on his forehead, but this was the door to healing, and he had to step through it—no matter how much it hurt.

She took his hand. "Tell me now. Tell me what's happening."

He shook his head and whispered. "I can't say. Please don't make me say."

There was a hint of the little boy in him now, in both his voice and the set of his shoulders. Once again he was becoming the child who remained crouched in the closet, terrified and grief-stricken.

"Race," she said. "This happened a long time ago. Remember that. You're all grown up. You're a man now, and you have nothing to fear."

He nodded and squared his shoulders. Only the single tear that trickled down his cheek gave away the pain he was feeling. "Okay."

"Now tell me."

He swallowed and said it in a strong clear voice. "He's cutting off her breasts. He's sawing them off with a hunting knife and there's blood everywhere."

"She's not feeling any pain, Race. You understand that, right?"

"Yes." But his fists were clenched, the cords in his neck standing out. "But…I want to stop him. I need to help her."

"But you can't, Race. You can't now because this happened years ago, and you couldn't then because you were just a little boy."

"I know." And then more softly. "I know."

"Has he stopped?"

"Yes. But he's holding…them. He's playing with them."

Candra felt sick. Of course the police report hadn't included this. They couldn't have known. "Tell me about it. Tell me what you see."

And he did. He spent the next several minutes describing things that she wished desperately he didn't have to say, that he'd never had to witness.

Suddenly his body slumped.

"What? What is it?"

He swallowed thickly. "He's gone. It's over."

If only that were true. "Not quite, Race. Stay and watch and tell me what you see."

"Why?"

"Just wait. You'll see."

And then he told her how the nine-year-old Race had waited until he heard the outer door close and then crept out of the closet. He'd stood at the end of the bed and stared at his mother for a long time, unmoving, tears streaming down his cheeks as he studied the woman he loved more than life itself. And then he made a decision.

He searched the room until he found the pieces of her that had been so casually discarded. He'd picked up her breasts and attempted to replace them on her chest. When they refused to stay he'd climbed onto the bloodied sheets beside her to hold them in place himself. He'd kissed her sweetly on the cheek and fallen asleep.

"And that's how the police found you," she told him a few minutes later when he'd shed his hypnotic state and been given a few moments to collect himself.

He had broken out in a cold sweat and was shivering. She fought the urge to hold him. If he asked, she would, but this was a very personal, private moment. She didn't want to breach any boundaries.

He nodded, teeth chattering. "I…I didn't remember…" He closed his eyes. "I didn't remember the rest."

"I know. You weren't ready to remember. It's…" She shook her head in wonder. "It's incredible that you've coped as well as you have. When Drew told me I couldn't believe it." She'd already explained how she'd come by the information and after an initial surge of anger, and an explanation that she was convinced it was essential in order to help him, he'd forgiven her.

Again he nodded, brushed away an errant tear. "I wanted to fix it. I couldn't stop him from doing it, so I thought…"

"I know." She fought tears of her own. "You were so brave. She would have been proud of you."

He looked at her then, met her gaze for the first time since she'd put him under. "I miss her."

She just nodded, reaching for him before she realized what she was doing.

But although she hadn't meant to, she didn't regret it. He eased into her arms as if he belonged there, resting his head on her shoulder, and holding on with a kind of trust and urgency that tugged at her heart.

"I'm tired," he said at last.

She eased herself back onto the pillows and urged him to lay his head on her lap. "Then sleep. I'll stay."

He nodded and within minutes had fallen into what she hoped would be a deep, dreamless, healing sleep.

Chapter Eleven

ဆ

The sun had reached its zenith and turned the full force of its heat upon them. It sparkled on the water and reflected in Candra's eyes, the light so intense as to be almost blinding. She stood with Race, hip-deep in the ocean, the waves lapping at their bodies, the water cooling their skin.

As always she was struck by his innate beauty. The classic line of his jaw, the windswept blond hair, the definition of his muscles. Even the scars that marred his skin added to the image, lending a sense of tragedy, a certain *mystique* to an already intriguing aura. And then there was his eyes—clear, gray and intense. Eyes that, at the moment, were shadowed by worry and uncertainty.

"I don't know about this," he said, looking around as if afraid they were being watched.

"This is a private beach. No one will bother us, or see us for that matter."

"That's not what I'm talking about. I just don't know if this…" he motioned to her and her scantily clad state, "is a good idea." She'd chosen her skimpiest bikini for the occasion, not that she'd be wearing it long. She hoped.

"Come on, Race. Don't cave on me now. We'll take it as slow as you like, and I'm hoping the water will act as a sort of…buffer to help you ease into the experience."

He licked his lips and nodded. This new vulnerability was at once endearing and disconcerting.

"Okay," he said. "Tell me what to do."

"Let's kneel down so the water is over our chests, all right?"

He agreed and a moment later their knees rested on the sand, chest to chest as the waves lapped gently around their shoulders.

"Good." She inched closer until her body was just inches from his. "How are you feeling?"

"I'm fine. *This* isn't the hard part."

"I know. But knowing it's coming can't be easy. Try not to focus on that. Just focus on me, okay?"

He nodded.

She lifted her face to his. "Kiss me."

He blinked, seemingly surprised by the suggestion.

"You don't have to go right for the steak, you know. You can start with an appetizer."

He laughed and she was glad. And then he framed her face in his hands and touched his lips to hers. The kiss was sweet, delicate, laced with a tenderness she hadn't noticed in him before. It sparked a need in her that ran so deep she didn't think she could trace its roots. When he fisted his hands in her hair and deepened the kiss she melted, became as liquid as the water that soothed their bodies. His tongue was both gentle and demanding, and he tasted of passion. And she knew she was lost.

She uttered a soft groan of pleasure and he broke the kiss to smile down at her.

He brushed some hair off her face and she asked. "Relaxed?"

"Yeah."

"Good. Now untie my top."

Tension seeped into his features, but he did as she asked. With hands that shook only a little he undid the strings that held her bikini in place. It came free and she allowed it to drift away on the waves, not caring where it went or if she ever found it again.

Race held her eyes, but then she was pleased to see his gaze drift downward.

She looked down to see what he was seeing. Her breasts were slightly distorted by the shifting waters, but still clearly visible. "Like what you see?"

"I don't know. I'm trying not to let myself feel anything."

"It's okay to feel. You have to or you won't move forward. *Feel*, but try to put those feelings into perspective. Now that you understand where the anxiety is coming from, it should be possible to set it aside."

He nodded again, his eyes riveted to her breasts. "Can I touch them?"

She wanted to laugh with relief, but managed to hold it in. "Of course. I would love for you to touch them."

Beneath the surface of the water he lifted his hand and brushed a fingertip along the under-curve of her breast. She watched his face, looking for a reaction.

He frowned a little and then lifted his other hand so that he was touching both breasts. And then he cupped them, and she wanted to swoon.

"Does that feel good?" he asked lifting his gaze to hers. "Is it okay?"

"Yes," she breathed. "God, yes. How—" She took a deep breath, trying to remain objective despite the heat that had begun coursing through her. "How are *you* feeling?"

"Okay, actually." He sounded surprised. "I'm a little tense, and I think my palms would be sweating, but it's hard to tell when they're under water."

"Right." She smiled, pleased that he was comfortable enough to make light of the situation. "Of course."

His touch became a little more firm, a little more assured. "They fit my hands well."

"Yes. They do." He needed all the affirmation she could give him. Not that she needed to embellish—not at all. "You can do more, touch more. Whenever you're ready."

He hesitated. "It's okay, right? It's okay to enjoy this."

She lifted a hand to his face, brushed her fingertips across light stubble. "Of course. You don't have to feel guilty about enjoying touching a woman's breasts. It's natural and right and—"

"And it's what she would have wanted."

She smiled her agreement. "Yes. She would have wanted you to be happy."

In response he took a deep breath and whisked his thumbs across her nipples.

"Oh. That's good. That's very good."

And then he palmed them, massaging them firmly and sending little waves of pleasure surging through her. She closed her eyes but was startled by the sound of his laughter. She opened her eyes to find him chuckling, his eyes smiling down on her.

"What?" she asked. "What's so funny?"

He shook his head. "I can't believe it."

"Believe what?"

"I just realized something, and it's just so ludicrous…"

She blew out a sigh of frustration. "Race?"

Suddenly he grasped her around the waist and stood, lifting her out of the water as he did so. He studied her breasts in the full light of the sun, tracing the curves, exploring, massaging. "I just realized part of the reason I was so nervous about touching them, why I was afraid. I thought—" He shrugged. "It's embarrassing."

"I won't laugh. I promise."

He licked his lips. "I think, way deep down, in the back of my mind…I think I was afraid they'd come off."

She smiled her sympathy and tamped down the chuckle that he didn't need to hear. "Oh, Race. That's perfectly understandable. In fact, it's wonderful."

His eyebrows arched. "*Wonderful*?"

"Of course it is. Now that you understand that you can let it go. With understanding comes release. And freedom."

He tweaked a nipple, the action firm and exciting. He bent low and whispered in her ear. "I'd like to taste you."

Shivers skittered down her arm. "Should we go back to the cottage?"

"No. On the sand, where it's warm and sunny. I want to see you." He straightened. "I want to see everything."

"All right." And then he scooped her up in his arms, and was splashing through the water toward the beach.

He laid her down on the sand, the heat of it seeping into her skin and the warmth of his gaze soaking into her soul. He lay beside her, his body nestled firmly against her but when he bent his head he surprised her. Rather than cover her breast with his lips, he took her mouth. Softly, sweetly, with such tenderness it made her want to cry. His hand cupped her rib cage, holding her firm, as if afraid she'd slip away.

Reluctantly, it seemed, he broke the kiss and peppered kisses along her jaw, and then down her throat. He traced his tongue over her collarbone and then across her chest until at last he reached the swell of aching flesh. His grip on her ribs tightened slightly, whether from excitement or anxiety she couldn't say, but the motion of his lips and tongue on her breast left no room for uncertainty. He tasted and suckled, all the while making soft noises of pleasure that reverberated through his chest and into her.

Gradually his mouth became more urgent, his grip on her more fierce. She laced her fingers through his hair in an effort to anchor herself to him and ease the need that had begun to build in her own loins. The warmth of the sand combined with the heat of his passion was enough to drive her to the brink of madness. But no matter what she wanted, or how much, she couldn't influence him. He had to take this at his own pace, make the most of the experience.

Just when she thought she'd burst from wanting him to go further he sat up, pushed her thighs apart and swung himself into position to kneel between them. And then, to her infinite frustration, he just sat there. Grinning at her.

"Well?" she prodded. "Aren't you going to do something?"

He traced a finger lightly along the edge of her bikini bottom. "Touch them for me. I want to see you touch your own breasts."

"Oh," she said, feeling a little breathless. "Okay." And then she cupped her own breasts and massaged her nipples between her fingers.

"Good. That's good." With his eyes burning a hole right through her, he reached for the ties on either side of her bikini, and tugged them open. Ever so gently, he laid the material down on the sand and, his eyes never leaving her, bent his head to taste her pussy. His tongue was soft and intimate, and then hot and aggressive.

He dipped inside her and she pinched her nipples to heighten her pleasure, arching her back and pushing her pussy more firmly against his mouth.

And then, abruptly, he was gone.

She opened her eyes to find him hovering above her, his gaze echoing the heat of the sun. "It's good," he said simply, and then he shed his swimsuit. He grasped her shoulders, rolled onto his back and dragged her on top of him. His hands bracketing her waist he held her firm, and when she offered him a breast, he took it hungrily.

She ground her pussy against the soft skin of his belly and threw her head back, allowing the sensations to wash over her.

It was more than the pleasure imparted by his mouth, or the heat of his skin against her sex. It was the knowledge that he was glorying in the experience as well, that he was as eager to receive pleasure as he was to give it, and that she was part of the reason for that. He had begun to heal and there was no greater pleasure for her than that.

"Christ," he said, his mouth abandoning her breasts at last. "This is incredible."

"It gets better," she teased, her hand reaching down to toy with his cock. "If you want it to."

"I want you to fuck me." He pushed her downward until his cock nudged her pussy and eased inside her. "I want you to fuck me while I watch you do it."

She braced her hands against the firm plane of his chest and proceeded to do exactly as he asked.

She rode him, taking him deep and fucking him hard, allowing her own passion to spill out and add its heat to the humid afternoon air. His hands cupped her breasts, continuing to explore and experience and soon he began to add his own thrusts to the rhythm of their lovemaking. He bracketed her hips and guided her, pounding her with his body until she thought she'd shatter from the pressure of it.

At last she touched herself, massaging her clit between two fingers, and when she came in a symphony of sound and color, he soon followed, arching his hips and roaring her name like a lion claiming his dominion.

And then, abruptly, she was on the sand again, the weight of his body pressing her firmly into the depression previously left by his body. He smiled at her, and brushed a strand of hair off her face. "You know," he said at last, "I just realized something."

"Yes?" She wriggled a little, wedging herself a little more firmly against him. "Realized what?"

"You're beautiful. In fact, I think you're the most beautiful woman I've ever seen."

Somehow, despite the way those words had stolen her breath, she found the strength to speak. "Ah, come on. You're just infatuated with my breasts. They're like a new toy for you."

He framed her face with his hands and held her there. "No. That's not it at all." And then he was kissing her and she knew she was lost.

* * * * *

A hundred meters down the beach, on the crest of an enormous sand dune, a pair of binoculars glinted in the sun.

Slowly, pensively, Anton lowered the binoculars from his eyes and laid them on the sand. He'd been patient and he'd been careful. It hadn't been difficult to find a man named Race who had been admitted to hospital with a gunshot wound, and from there tracing his movements had been child's play. The difficulty had come with the fact that he was never alone, and his constant state of being surrounded by people had thwarted several of Anton's plans to rid himself of the mysterious pest. But then, he and this woman had secluded themselves in this seaside cottage. It was out of the way and isolated. And, at last, it seemed, Anton's diligence was going to pay off.

Now he just had to come up with a plan that would sate both his need for revenge and his craving for sexual satisfaction. This man was dangerous, that much was obvious, and he had to be approached with caution.

He also needed to be taught a lesson before he died, and teaching lessons was something Anton excelled at.

In fact, it was what he lived for.

A sly smile on his lips, he slunk back down the dune and headed to his car. A plan had begun to take shape in his mind, but he wanted to take his time and make sure he did it right. This time there could be no room for error.

Chapter Twelve

ঙ

Race's senses came awake slowly, one by one.

First, he became aware of the distant sound of the surf. The wind must have picked up today because the water no longer lapped gently at the beach, but pounded it, each wave crashing against the sand like an angry fist. But beneath the tumult that raged outside he heard the soft breathing of the woman beside him.

He could smell her, too. The scent of her soap and shampoo had faded, leaving behind only a light sweetness that mingled with the mustiness of sleep and last night's sex.

He rolled over and touched her, draping his arm across her waist and drawing her close so that her back snuggled against his chest and her behind nestled against his early morning erection.

His fingertips drifted over her skin, savoring the warmth, the velvety softness and the sweet little mewling sounds she made in her sleep. He reached a breast and tentatively touched the soft curve of flesh. His caress was gentle but assured, light yet confident. He felt no trepidation, no anxiety. No longer did he have this sense of some nameless threat, no nervous pit of fear gnawed in his gut. He felt only warmth and pleasure and a renewed sense of wonder that life could still hold surprises. He'd had surprises in his life, certainly, but his last moments of joyous wonder had occurred in childhood. He'd thought the days of happy surprises had died along with days of ice-cream sundaes and birthday candles.

He was glad to be proved wrong.

He still marveled at it. At the change in him, as well as the change in how he felt about her. Originally he'd seen her as a threat. She'd wanted to scratch away at walls that he'd spent years constructing. She wanted to see things that he'd tried so hard to keep hidden. He'd feared her.

Looking back now, however, he had to admit that perhaps it wasn't her he had feared so much as the knowledge—the certainty—that he *would* tell her those things. He'd been afraid of his own vulnerability, a vulnerability that only she could see.

And now she'd ceased being a threat. She'd turned from therapist to friend, from consultant to lover. If, of course, she'd ever truly been those things. He had a sense that there had always been more between them.

But although he wasn't certain of their beginning, he was certain of their present.

He cared for her, trusted her. He trusted her more than he'd ever trusted anyone. But could he trust her enough?

At last he indulged himself and opened his eyes. Sunlight streamed in the windows, highlighting the red in her hair and the creamy bronze of her skin. He gave in to impulse and pressed a kiss to her shoulder.

She stirred and rolled over and when she opened her eyes and looked up at him he almost felt as if she could see right through him, see everything, right down to his last remaining secrets. Secrets that even he wanted to hide from.

He threw off the covers and erupted from the bed.

"Race?"

He stalked to the patio door that looked out over the water. He whipped aside the sliding glass door and savored the breeze that ruffled his hair. He wanted to step outside, but something held him back.

"Race, what is it?"

She stood behind him. He could feel her. He could feel her as surely as he could feel the new and terrifying fear that had begun to take root in his gut. The fear of losing something he cared about. The fear of it, and the certainty. The only uncertainty — the only question was, would he lose her to the evils that lurked in the shadows? Or to the evil that lurked in his own soul?

Her fingers skimmed up his back. "I hope you slept well. You certainly should have after yesterday."

They'd made love through the afternoon, and well into the night. They'd kissed and touched and explored, tenderly, sweetly, completely. He'd sighed over the exquisiteness of her and the way her touch had seeped through his skin and beyond. He'd cradled her and cared for her, soothed and stroked. He'd been the gentle, attentive lover, but now, looking out over the ocean and seeing the violence of the wind and the water, he acknowledged the violence in him.

And felt it stir.

He reached for her, grabbed her by the shoulders and dragged her to him.

"Race?" she asked, suddenly breathless. "What are you doing?"

His kiss was his answer.

Everything inside her went on alert. He'd never kissed her like this before. His mouth was hungry, his embrace fierce, the kiss more assault than seduction. He fisted his hands in her hair and held her firm as he plundered her mouth and pressed his cock against her naked belly. He pushed her back against the door and, one hand still holding her head, his other slid between her thighs. He pushed inside her, two fingers, perhaps three, so hard and so deep that she threw her head back, knocking her skull against the glass even as she gasped for breath.

The suddenness and intensity of his onslaught at once startled and excited her. She was wet, her skin already slicked with sweat, but concern won out over lust, and she found the strength to push him away. She planted both hands on his chest and heaved. It was like pushing against solid rock. But he relented and released her.

Her breath rasping hot in her lungs, she looked at him. Abruptly the breath caught in her throat. His eyes burned with something—something raw and fierce. Something she'd never seen before.

"Wh-what the hell do you think you're doing?" She stepped away from the door, stopping in the middle of the room. She wiped at her lips, already sore and bruised, and felt a few beads of moisture slip down the insides of her thighs.

He moved closer. "Are you saying you don't want it? You don't want me?"

She took a step back. "That's ridiculous. I wanted you all day yesterday. I just don't want you like this."

"You want me? Then you want all of me, and *this* is part of me."

"I don't know what you're talking about. I—" He moved so quickly she didn't have time to react. He grabbed her, swept her up in his arms and threw her onto the bed, landing on top of her. "Race! What—"

He cut off her words with a kiss. Hot and hard, his mouth pressed to hers, the weight of his body held her immobile. He grabbed her hands, latched his fingers around her wrists, making her capture complete.

His mouth moved to her throat, teeth sank into skin, his bite hard enough that it verged on the delicate knife-edge between pain and pleasure. She squirmed, fighting him and her own reactions to him. How could something feel so wrong and so right at the same time?

He moved to her breast, latched onto it and sucked—hard. She arched against him, seeking both pleasure and release. He moved to the other breast and she sucked in a dose of oxygen.

"Get off," she pleaded, although she knew her voice lacked conviction.

He raised his head and looked at her.

"Are you going to take me against my will?" she continued, gathering strength. "Is that what this is about?"

His eyes were haunting, his voice full of heat. "Do you want me to stop? If you tell me to stop now—and mean it—I will."

She licked her lips, her flesh held captive by his body, her soul held hostage by his gaze. "What *is* this about? I think I should know."

He leaned forward and whispered slowly, "Do you want me to stop?"

She waited, debating with herself. In the end she said nothing, lover won out over therapist and she knew there was no turning back.

He took her mouth again then. His tongue thrust deeply into her mouth as his hands released her wrists and gripped her roughly around the waist. He stood, pulling her toward him as he did so. When her legs were hanging over the side of the bed, he pushed her knees apart and stepped between them.

His thrust was sudden and deep, quick and hard. He gripped her hips, his fingertips sinking into her and holding her steady against his onslaught. Breathless, and needing something to anchor herself to, she grabbed his wrists and hung on.

"Look at me," he said, his words a command although his voice was little more than a whisper.

She complied. She opened her eyes and met his gaze. The feral intensity in him never wavered, the sense of barely contained brutality. With every thrust of his cock she felt it, like little shockwaves through her soul.

He reached around and gripped her ass, squeezing so that she gripped him even more tightly. Still he held her eyes and she lost herself there. Her arousal spiraled higher, driven as much by the physical as by the emotional.

A climax loomed. Just on the edges of her senses she could feel it, growing, taking shape like a monster rising up out of the dark. She arched her back and closed her eyes and gave herself over to it.

"Open your eyes!" Race grabbed her by the shoulders and hauled her up to a seated position. Her eyes flew open just as the monster's teeth sank into her.

He didn't relent, continuing to fuck her as the contractions seized her and stole her breath.

Abruptly he stopped, made one last vicious thrust and came, letting out a primal cry and arching his back as it pumped through him.

He sealed his mouth to hers in a fierce kiss before falling onto the bed and dragging her down to lie beside him.

It took her several moments to gather her wits about her, but when she turned to him, her mind full of questions, she was surprised to find that he had already fallen asleep.

* * * * *

"Here." Candra set an enormous mug of steaming coffee onto the cedar rail at Race's elbow.

"Thanks." He picked it up and sipped, his eyes never moving from the horizon he'd been studying for the past half hour.

The wind had calmed a bit, but whitecaps still dotted the waves here and there, and the breeze flirted with their hair. But the peacefulness of the setting did nothing to ease the anxiety that had been gnawing in Candra's gut ever since the scene in the bedroom.

He'd awoken sullen and silent and when pressed had said only that he needed to tell her something, and that he'd like to have some food in his stomach before he did so.

They'd eaten omelets and toast in silence, and now, with this last cup of coffee, she could only assume he would finally reveal whatever it was he needed to reveal.

She stood beside him, leaning against the rail, watching him sip. And waiting.

She felt ready, braced for whatever he would tell her, but nothing could have prepared her for the next words out of his mouth.

"I've killed, Candra. I've killed more than fifteen men." He turned to look at her. "And I fully intend to do it again."

She opened her mouth to speak, and then abruptly closed it again. And then she laughed.

"You don't believe me."

The tone of his voice and the look in his eyes stole the laughter from her lips. "No. Of course I don't. Why are you doing this? Are you trying to shock me? Show me some brutal side of you and then tell me something horrible just to get me to walk away from you? Well, it won't work, Race. I'm here for the long haul. I'm—"

He gripped her by the shoulders and shook her. "I'm not lying, dammit!" He stopped, dropped his hands from her shoulders and took a step back, almost as if he'd startled himself with his own reaction. "It's the truth. I've put a gun to the backs of their heads and I've slit their throats. I've killed them quick, and I've killed them slow. I've beat them senseless and then watched their blood seep out of them into the ocean as they pleaded with me to let them live."

Candra stared at him for a moment and then pulled her terrycloth robe a little more tightly about her. Suddenly the air had taken on a distinct chill. "Why are you doing this? What do you want from me?"

"I want you to understand. I want you to know all of me." He turned away from her, back to the ocean and its inherent desolation. "God knows why, but I need for you to know all of me. If you walk away, so be it. But I need you to know."

She wanted to move away but she held her ground. "Well then...finish it. Tell me the rest."

He looked at her.

"Tell me *why* you killed them." She still didn't believe it. Couldn't believe it. But she knew she had to play this out or they'd get nowhere.

"You won't believe me."

She blinked in astonishment. "You tell me you've killed, that you've committed murder, and now you're saying that there's something even *more* fantastic? Even more unbelievable? Come on, Race. If you really—"

"I see things."

Confused, she leaned back against the rail. "What kinds of things?"

He took a deep breath and shook his head, trained his gaze on the whitecaps that dotted the waves and the seagulls that wheeled overhead. "I was seventeen. The first time was...overwhelming. Horrifying. I had no idea what was happening, and was convinced I was dying." He raked his fingers through his hair. "And then later I wished I could have."

Understanding glimmered. "Your episodes. This is about those…seizures that you have."

He nodded, swallowed and continued.

"It was at the last foster home that I lived in. The family was good, the best I'd lived with. And for once I felt like I could be happy. I stopped skipping school and getting into fights. I felt like I had a handle on things. And although the parents were largely to thank, they weren't the main reason." His fingers gripped the railing. "They had a daughter. She was a year or so younger than me, but mature beyond her years. She was smart and pretty and had this…energy about her."

"You fell in love with her."

He chuckled, but his knuckles were white. "Yes. But not in the way that you think. She was, in the truest sense, like a sister to me. We did things together, talked about things, personal things. She grounded me, somehow. Made me feel smart and special, and like I had a place."

"She sounds special."

"She was. Linnea was, in the truest sense of the word, an angel."

"Was. She died."

"Yes. And I could have stopped it, and didn't."

Candra cradled her mug in her hands. "I find that hard to believe."

"You don't understand. I— Fuck!" He shook his head again, turned and walked away. When he turned around again confusion and anger clouded his expression. "I've never told *anyone* this before, and with good reason. Any sane person would immediately call the men in the little white coats and cart me away. Either that or the police. Either way my life is over." Suddenly he laughed, the sound strained. "But then again, maybe I never had a life in the first place."

She crossed the deck and grasped his hand. "I won't do either of those things, Race. I won't call you crazy and I won't call the cops. You must trust me or you wouldn't have come this far."

"What about Drew? How can you not tell him?"

"I just won't. You're telling me this in confidence. It goes no further."

"So I'm your patient again, is that it?" His voice had taken on an edge.

"No," she said, admitting it at last to him, as much as to herself. "You aren't now, and you never were, Race. You're more than that. God help me, but you're so much more."

He studied her for a moment, but apparently decided to believe her. He moved back to the rail, leaned against it for support and continued. "It happened one Friday night. I was in my room reading when it hit. At first it was like someone had smacked me, slapped me hard across the face. My head literally whipped to the side, and when I opened my eyes I couldn't believe there was no one there. But then I felt it again, and I lost my vision completely. Everything went black and I had only the vaguest sense of motion and voices around me. I tried to call out, but couldn't. I was alone in my room, writhing on the bed, fighting off some invisible attacker as they punched and kicked and eventually stabbed me."

She caught her breath. "Stabbed you?"

"Yes." He grabbed her hand and squeezed. "I felt the knife go into my stomach as clearly as you feel my hand on yours right now." He let go. "And then I felt it slice across my throat. I even felt the blood come gushing out. It was warm and sticky, and I felt it soak into my clothes. And I remember thinking, 'This is it. I'm dying and I don't even know why.'

But then, just as I felt myself go weak and I could barely breathe, it stopped." He took a sip of coffee, and she noticed that the cup shook a little in his hand. "I opened my eyes and found myself alone in my room. I was drenched in sweat, but other than that, unscathed. I remember looking at the clock and noting that it was 11:35."

When he didn't continue, she prodded. "Did you tell anybody?"

"No. I assumed it had been a horrible dream, and discounted it. But it haunted me all the next day. I couldn't eat, felt nauseous and anxious all the time. And then, the next night Linnea was at the door, getting ready to go out on a date."

"Oh," she breathed. "No."

"When I saw her at the door, I *knew*. I just knew that she was the one who was going to be attacked, and that I should stop her. I tried. I came up with some lame excuse about needing her to help with homework or…whatever, but she just laughed at me, hugged me and kissed me on the cheek. When her date came to the door and I saw him…" His fists clenched into balls of angry flesh. "I knew he was the one. I had this vision of wrapping my hands around his throat and squeezing until his eyes rolled back and he struggled for air that would never come."

His words gave her chills, but she said nothing.

"I ended up doing nothing. I hoped I was wrong. I convinced myself that it was crazy, and that I was just suffering from some hormonal overload or something. But I sweated that whole night. I lay in my room, stared at the ceiling and sweated. And when she missed her curfew and didn't show up at midnight, I knew it was already too late. They found her in the basement of the movie theater. He'd sneaked her down there, turned out the lights, and when she said no, he'd decided she needed some persuading. Not that any of that matters. He beat her and stabbed her. Her hand had been slammed against the concrete floor and her watch broke. It said 11:15 — the time that I felt the first blow the night before. She died and it was my fault."

"Race." She placed a hand on his arm. "That's ridiculous. It wasn't your fault."

He ripped his arm out of her grip and stalked away. "I didn't stick the knife in her, but I may as well have. I should have tackled her to the ground and kept her from going! Or...or...I should have followed them and made sure she was all right." He kicked a deck chair that had the misfortune of being in front of him. It flew out onto the beach, landing in a crumpled heap.

"But I didn't do any of that. I ignored what I *knew* to be the truth, and she paid the price." He turned to look at her. "But I never let that happen again. The next time it happened I understood. I knew what was happening, and I knew that I had a chance — no, I had an *obligation* to do something about it."

She shook her head, still confused. "I don't understand. What are you saying?"

He stepped closer, grabbed her hands, his expression now earnest, his voice compelling. "I'd been given a gift. A jagged, painful gift, perhaps, but still, a gift. After a few more episodes and watching the papers I figured it out." He released her and stepped back. "I was living their death with them. I experienced their beatings, saw things through their eyes, and all exactly twenty-four hours before the actual events. Those hours gave me time to figure out who they were and how it happened. And then that gave me a way to make sure it didn't."

"So..." She blinked as understanding dawned. "So *that's* why you went to that cemetery? That's how you knew?"

His face fell. "Yes. But that time I didn't have enough to go on, and I got there too late. It happens sometimes. And it just about kills me when it does."

"But let me get this straight. You get there, stop the attack…" She licked her lips. "And then what?"

"I tranquilize both the victim and assailant. I leave the victim at the scene and take away her attacker."

Her mouth was dry. She didn't want to say it, but knew she had to. "And you don't turn them in to police, do you?"

"No. They don't deserve that kind of consideration, and what cop would believe me anyway? They'd label me a lunatic and stick me in an asylum. Not to mention the fact that it leaves the possibility that these men might get out and do it again. I don't like uncertainties where women's safety is concerned."

She whispered, "So you kill them."

"Yes." His voice was dead, his eyes cold. "I kill them and dispose of the body so that they're never found. And it's a lot easier than you might think." And with that he turned and walked away.

He headed down the beach as she stood there in stunned silence and watched him go.

Chapter Thirteen

ନ୍ତ

Candra settled down on the beach beside him and hugged her knees. A wave broke over the sand and crept up the beach to sip at her toes. She set her gaze on the horizon but when she'd sat down she'd taken note of the rigid set of his jaw, the lines of tension in his forehead.

"Shall I pack up?" he asked when several moments had passed. "Physically I'm fine. There's no reason I can't—"

"What happened to him?"

He turned to her, blinked. "What? Who?"

"The man who killed Linnea. Did he go to prison?"

His jaw flexed, fists clenched. "No. They didn't have enough physical evidence to prosecute and he had several people swearing they'd seen them have a fight and he'd left halfway through the movie."

"And what happened to him?"

"I didn't go after him, if that's what you're asking."

"Why not?"

"Because as certain as I was, I never actually saw his face in my vision, and I didn't catch him in the act. There was a small chance I could be wrong, and as unlikely as that was, I couldn't take that risk."

She considered that for a moment then nodded. "I see."

"Oh? And what, exactly, do you see?"

She turned to face him then, studied him intently before laying a hand on his arm and saying, "I see a good man. A man who has done the best he could with the cards he's been dealt. You did what you thought you had to do, Race, and I can't fault you for that. Whether or not I agree with your methods, I can't fault your motives." She squeezed. "Or your ultimate mission."

"But?"

"But you have to stop."

He looked at her for a moment, then shook his head and stood, stared out over the water. He laughed. "I should have known. Good God, of course."

She felt a little heat creep into her cheeks. She rose to her feet as well. "Of course what?"

"Of course you'd put on the old morality cape. Suddenly you're a crusader for all that's right and good, is that it?"

"Are you implying that I don't live my life that way?"

He leaned in close enough that she could smell the coffee on his breath and see the fire smoldering in his eyes. "You fuck men for money. *You* do the math."

She felt a few embers spark to life herself and plowed a palm against his chest. "You son of a bitch! How dare you? You know full well I—" She stopped herself, refusing to justify herself to him and taking a moment to take stock of the situation. She took a deep breath. "No. I won't go there. You're feeling angry and vulnerable and—"

"Oh, for God's sake, stop it. Stop with the psychobabble crap! Don't talk *at* me, talk *to* me."

"Well, then you stop venting *at* me and talk like the intelligent man I know you are."

His fists clenched and his chest heaved. "I can't stop. How the hell can I stop? What? Am I just supposed to stand by and let them die? *I can't do that!* I did it once, you can't possibly ask me to do it again."

"Then go to the police. Tell them what you've seen. Let them handle it."

"That's a load of bullshit and you know it."

"Why? Why is it bullshit?"

"It's bullshit because in the first place, they'd never believe me. And in the second place—"

He grunted, clutched at his shoulder, staggered backward and fell to his knees, gasping for breath.

She rushed to him, reaching him just as an unseen force toppled him to the side. She fell to her knees beside him, touching a hand to his cheek. His skin felt cold and clammy, his breath came in harsh gasps.

"Race?" She brushed a thumb across his cheekbone. "Jesus, Race. How can I help?"

He didn't respond. His eyes remained wide, staring, unfocused, his body rigid, but every once in a while his face would contort, his body jerk in small, intense spasms.

She lost track of time, focusing only on Race and his struggle. She kept saying his name over and over, stroking his cheek, wishing desperately that it would stop and cursing a god that would inflict such horrors on his minions.

"Good God, Race," she whispered, "how can you have lived with this for so long?"

And then, abruptly, his eyes focused. He looked at her, reached for her and said her name. She grasped his hand just as his back arched, his eyes rolled back in his head and he let out a soul-piercing scream.

His hand fell to the sand, his eyes closed and his body went limp. He didn't open his eyes again.

"Race?" she cried, terrified. "Wake up!" He didn't stir, but he was breathing and a quick check of his carotid confirmed that his pulse was rapid but strong. Drained and exhausted, she collapsed. She draped herself over him protectively, sobbing and allowing the tears of helpless rage to soak into the sand.

* * * * *

Candra set the mug of steaming tea on the nightstand and sat down on the bed beside him. She touched his forehead and was amazed when he didn't bat her hand away. His skin was cool but clammy, no doubt thanks to the exhausting trek back up the beach to the cottage. He'd finally awoken, but had been as weak as a kitten, needing to lean heavily on her in order to make it across the paltry hundred meters of sand to the door.

His eyes remained closed.

"I made some tea. Something warm in your stomach will help." When he didn't respond, she touched his cheek. "Race? Are you awake?"

Suddenly his hand flew up and caught her by the wrist. He pressed her palm to his lips and kissed it. Eyes still closed he said, "You have to get out of here. We both do. And we have to go as soon as possible."

"Race, you're in no shape to go anywhere. Besides, if you're planning on going to that damn apartment and tracing down another killer then you can just—"

"No." At last he opened his eyes but they were dull. "No, I don't have to do that. Not this time."

She blinked, slightly confused by his choice of words. "What do you mean?"

"I don't have to do that because I know exactly who the victim is, and where it happens."

The way he was looking at her—the intensity of his gaze, and the passion behind his words, combined to send a shiver skittering down her spine. "What is it?" she whispered. "You're scaring me."

"Good. I hope so." He closed his eyes again, took a deep breath. "Because it happens here, on the beach. And the victim is you, Candra. And the way I'm feeling now, I can't do a thing to stop it." He opened his eyes, his grip on her hand tightening. "So we have to get out. God knows I've never run from anything, but this time…" He shook his head. "This time is different. I've never felt like this before."

She brushed her fingers through his hair. "Different how? You're not usually affected like this?"

"No. I've never passed out like that. I usually wake up a little weak from the pain, but I recover in minutes. And that's not all. The vision was…" His voice trailed away, his eyes closed. "It was bizarre because the feelings, the pain, it was all so intense, and yet it was hazy, too. Like I was watching it all through a fog. I could *feel* but I couldn't *see*."

"And usually you see very clearly?"

"Yes. If the victim's eyes aren't covered, everything is clear. Crystal-clear. Almost more vivid than what I see with my own eyes."

"Like an intense dream?"

He opened his eyes. "Yes. Like a nightmare."

"So if you couldn't see, how do you know it was here?"

"I just do. I…heard things. Felt things. I just know. And I know we have to get out."

"Race, I—"

He gripped her hand, squeezed. "I hate it, hate myself for it, but if I have to run and hide like a little boy in a closet all over again in order to keep you safe, that's exactly what I'll do."

There was something—something about his words, and the way he was looking at her. It drew her in, made her breath catch. "You won't get any arguments from me. Leaving doesn't make you a coward. It makes you smart. We can leave as soon as you're strong enough."

"I'm just used to taking care of things myself. To being the one to fix things. It's hard to let go of that."

"It's okay. It's the right thing to do."

But he didn't seem to hear her. His grip on her hand tightened. "I can't risk losing this, Candra. I can't risk losing *you*."

She smiled, trying to shrug off the tightening in her chest. "Come on, now. You're gonna get me all misty."

"I mean it. You're the best thing that's ever happened to me. I think…" But he stopped there, closed his mouth, and dropped his gaze. The unspoken words hung between them. But remained unspoken.

She leaned in and kissed him, gently, sweetly. "We'll go as soon as you're ready. Rest a little bit longer and I'll make us something to eat. Something in your stomach should help."

He nodded and settled back into the pillow. "Okay. Thanks."

When he seemed settled and his breathing eased, she got up and walked to the kitchen. When she got there she leaned back against the counter, pressed a hand to her tummy and willed her pulse to slow. The combination of anxiety and fear, excitement and hopefulness made a potent mix, a mix that she'd never experienced before, and she wasn't sure what to do with it.

She couldn't be a hundred percent sure of the words that he'd left unsaid, but she could suspect. Mainly because they echoed her own sentiments. Sentiments not even she had the courage to voice aloud.

She knew one thing, however. Like Race, she'd found something good, and intended to do everything in her power to keep it.

* * * * *

"Hey, sweets."

Megan looked up from her desk and smiled. "Hi."

Drew strode into the outer office, cocky grin in place and swaggering like only a cop with fifteen years under his belt could swagger. It was all a show, though, she knew. Underneath he was soft as a teddy bear, and twice as cuddly. Or at least she imagined he was.

Impatient with herself, she tapped her keyboard and closed off her word file before swiveling to face him. "What can I do for you, officer?" Her voice came out much harsher than she intended.

His face fell. "Officer? That's awfully formal, don't you think?"

She softened her tone, made a joke out of it. "Well, I'm a formal kinda gal."

His brown eyes appraised her. "Uh-huh."

"You don't believe me?"

"I believe you're exactly as formal, or *informal* as you need to be."

Intrigued, she leaned back in her chair and laced her fingers together. "I'm not sure if I should be flattered or insulted."

"Well—"

Eric burst into the outer office. "Meg! Can you please—" He drew up short, his eyes homing in on Drew. "Oh." He gathered himself together and extended a hand. "Hello, Andrew."

"Eric." Drew shook his hand but the gesture was brief and left pained expressions on both men's faces. Like little boys who had just been forced to sample brussels sprouts. Megan smiled in spite of herself.

Eric dropped a file on Megan's desk. "Would you mind calling Dantrell and asking him to check into these sales figures? I'd like a second opinion before I rake my newest VP over the coals."

She reached for the file. "Sure. I'll call right away."

"Thanks." Eric turned to go, but hesitated. "Was there something you wanted? Or are you just here to distract my assistant?" He said it with a grin, but nothing could hide the tension behind his words.

Drew cocked his head and replied lazily. "Actually I do have some official business. Distracting Meg is just a…perk." He winked her way and she found that she was enjoying the attention—a little too much.

"Okay," replied Eric. "Can we get on with it, then? I have a very full schedule."

Megan knew full well he intended to slip out early and head to the spa for a massage and manicure.

"I wondered if you'd heard anything from Candra and Race."

"You have her cell number," said Eric. "Why don't you call her yourself?"

"She's turned it off and she neglected to give me the number for the cottage."

"Neglected?" asked Eric. "Or refused?"

"Is there something wrong?" asked Megan, suddenly concerned.

"No. Nothing specific. It's just that it's been a couple of weeks and…" Drew shrugged. "I've always felt a little bit responsible for Candra. And now, with a killer on the loose…"

"Hmm." Eric crossed his arms. "Well, I can assure you they're fine. Race can look out for her just fine. Even if he is a *suspect* in your whacked-out murder investigation."

"Race was *shot*, for chrissake. He's in no condition to tackle a raging gerbil, let alone protect Candra from a psychopathic killer."

"Boys, *boys*!" Megan stood and placed a hand on each tense forearm, but before she could continue, the cell phone in Drew's pocket chimed loudly.

With a scathing glance at Eric, he shook off her arm and excused himself to step away and take the call.

She leaned close to Eric and whispered, "What is *with* you two anyway?"

"He insulted Race."

"He did not. You're just determined to take offense to everything he says."

"That's because most of what he says is *offensive*!"

She rolled her eyes. "Well, try and behave, will you? For my sake."

Drew turned off his phone and joined them again, his brows pulled together, his gaze intense. He spoke to Megan. "Do you have the number for the cottage?"

She blinked, startled by the urgency of his tone. "Yes, but—"

"But if Candra didn't want you to have it, I don't see why *we* should give it to you."

Drew ignored Eric, keeping his gaze trained on Megan. "It's imperative that I get hold of her, Megan."

"Why? What's happened?"

He grasped her hand. "I just received some new information and I need to speak to Race about it. To both of them." He squeezed. "Please. I don't want to have to send a squad car up there to get them."

She nodded, reading both sincerity and urgency in his eyes. "All right. Just give me a minute to get my purse."

Chapter Fourteen

ജ

The water was hot, the bathroom already full of steam by the time Candra stepped into the shower. She bent her head, allowing the water to pound her skull and sluice down her skin. She breathed in heat and moisture and imagined it cleansing her soul as well as her lungs. The rage, however, remained.

Every time she thought of Race and the curse he'd had to live with, of the horrors he'd witnessed and the struggles he'd had to endure, her pulse raced and her blood simmered in her veins. Seeing him so weak and exhausted that he barely had the strength to eat added fuel to the flames.

After choking down a few morsels of chicken and bread just to appease her, he'd sat up and tried to get out of bed. He'd wanted to leave as soon as possible, but one glimpse of him standing beside the bed, gripping a bedpost in what was obviously a desperate search for balance, had her pushing him back onto the mattress. They still had more than twenty hours, didn't they? There was no reason he couldn't get a decent night's sleep, and hopefully be more able to cope in the morning.

He'd argued with her but she'd insisted, and in the end her tenacity, combined with his weakened state, had won out. Propped up on pillows he'd watched television for a time but soon his eyelids had drooped and about twenty minutes ago he'd finally fallen asleep again.

This couldn't last, she reasoned with herself. He'll be better in the morning.

He had to be.

She had just reached for the shampoo when the trill of the cordless phone interrupted her reverie.

Cursing modern "conveniences", but unable to ignore the summons, she turned off the water and quickly stepped out of the stall. Dripping and shivering she picked up the phone.

"Hello?" she snapped. "What do you want?"

"Well, top o'the mornin' to you too."

Sighing, she reached for a thick terrycloth robe. "Oh. Hi, Drew." She slipped an arm into the sleeve. "First of all it's not morning, and second of all, you're not Irish."

"Firstly, my great-grandfather on my father's side came from Dublin."

"Uh-huh." She slipped on the other sleeve and wrapped the belt around her.

"And secondly, the sound of your voice is as bright and cheery as the sight of the morning sun breaking over the horizon."

"Okay, spill it. What's wrong?"

He cleared his throat. "Wrong?"

"Yes. You're never this cheerful and I can only surmise that that means you have something horrible to tell me and are having trouble working up the nerve to do it."

"I have cheerful…moments," he argued.

"*Drew.*" Because her knees suddenly felt weak, she plunked down on the toilet seat. "Tell me."

His silence confirmed her worst fears. "I don't want to talk about it over the phone. I'd like to come up there to see you. To see both of you."

"Is this about the case?"

"Yes."

She felt sick. "You're going to arrest Race, aren't you? I won't have it, Drew. If I have to—"

"Candra! It's nothing like that."

She stopped, took a deep breath. "Okay. What is it, then?"

"I'll just say that Race is no longer a suspect, but that some evidence has come to light that he needs to be made aware of."

"What kind of evidence?"

"Not on the phone, Candra. I need to see him in person."

"Is it about his mother?"

"Candra, please."

"It's not good, is it? It's going to be hard for him to hear."

Several seconds passed before he answered. "Yes. Very hard."

She stared at the door, envisioned Race in bed. Pale and weak and, for perhaps the first time in his life, completely vulnerable. Whatever it was Drew had in store for him, he was in no shape to hear it. "Okay, Drew. We'll meet, but not here. Race and I are coming back to the city tomorrow morning, and once I get him settled at Eric's, I'll meet with you and you can tell me what this is all about." Eric would take care of him and God knew she'd be safe with Drew.

"You? Candra, I need to discuss this with *him*."

"You'll tell me first and let me decide how to present it to him, or you won't see him for days. Maybe never."

"What? What the hell was that, Candra? A threat?"

"Take it as you will. It's the simple truth. Race isn't feeling well and I'm not going to jeopardize his state of mind further by subjecting him to any unnecessary emotional trauma."

"Is it the gunshot wound? Does he need medical attention?"

"No, no. Nothing like that. Just trust me, Drew. I know what I'm doing."

Water dripped from the faucet in the shower and outside the wind had picked up once again. A tree branch clicked against the window and when Drew spoke again his voice was low and thoughtful. "All right. I'll go along with it, but only because I've known you for ten years. But you have to assure me that he will be told eventually."

"Of course." In her own time and in her own way.

"All right. Come to the station tomorrow at three?"

"Fine." Race's vision had occurred at four p.m., so surely he'd have no objections to her being safely stashed away in a police station at that time. "I'll see you then."

She clicked off the phone and stared at it, cradled snugly in her palm. What could it be? What could possibly be so disturbing that even Drew would acknowledge its possible impact on Race's state of mind? And was she naïve to think that even someone who cared for him as much as she did could possibly dull the blow?

* * * * *

Anton sat in his truck and stared at the house with the soaring rooftops and stained glass windows. He stared at it, studied it, trying to place it. He'd seen that house before, he was certain of it. But he'd never been in this end of the city before, so how could he—

And then it hit him.

He'd never been here, but he'd seen pictures. There had been an entire album full of photographs of this house. He'd found it when he'd been going through Race's apartment looking for clues as to his identity and whereabouts. Anton had come across the album and the first photo had been so arresting he'd given in to the urge to flip to the next. And the next, and the next. He'd been amazed by what he found. Intrigued. Aroused. His fascination had been so complete that he'd even gone so far as to scan the floor plan that he'd found tucked in the back of the album.

And now he was so very glad he had. His little pigeon had settled in here to roost, and the possibilities were endless. Anton's palms began to sweat in anticipation, and a smile twisted his lips as the fantasies poured through him.

For as long as he could remember, violence had excited him. It was about power, but it was about so much more. Screams of pain and the smell of blood were as intoxicating as a narcotic, and it had been too long since his last fix. But satisfaction was at hand.

It wouldn't be long now.

* * * * *

"Here ya go, buddy."

Race opened his eyes and squinted against the late afternoon sun. Eric towered over his lounge chair, holding out a beer, and sporting an affable grin. His eyes, however told another story.

Race hated seeing that kind of concern in his friend's eyes, even more than he'd hated seeing it in Candra's. But, unfortunately, he lacked the energy to set them straight and assure them that he was fine and they should stop worrying about him. Ironically, he found he even lacked the energy to work up a good froth about it at all.

He had awoken that morning feeling better, but his energy level was still lacking. Normally he would have dived into that pool and done fifty laps just to work out the kinks.

Now the thought of dangling his feet in the water made him tired.

He sat up and accepted the beer. "Has Candra called?"

"No," said Eric, plopping himself down on a neighboring chair. "She only left ten minutes ago. Give it another fifteen before you start to worry. Man, this flu bug you've got has really got you in a tailspin, doesn't it?"

"I just don't like it. That cop who picked her up looked awfully young." On Race's insistence, Drew had agreed to send a squad car to pick Candra up and transport her to the station.

"That's because he was young. But whatever it is has got you so spooked and worried about her, I'm sure he can handle it. He may have been young, but he also had a gun and biceps like Mahatma Ghandi."

Race paused, considered, and then snorted in laughter, barely refraining from spraying his beer all over the patio. "Ghandi? He had biceps like fuckin' *Ghandi*?"

"Oops," laughed Eric. "Did I say that? I meant Muhammad Ali." He pointed a finger. "But it got a laugh out of ya. Didn't it, my taciturn friend?"

Race rolled his eyes, but knew it was pointless to deny it.

"She's fine," assured Eric. "Whatever it is has got you so worried, I'm sure it's nothing. Sergeant Dickless will have her back safe and sound in no time."

Race cocked an eyebrow. "Sergeant Dickless? As in Drew? What have you got against him, anyway?"

"Nothing." Eric examined his beer. "Nothing at all." Abruptly he launched from the deck chair. "But I do have something against tough steaks. I'm going inside and get those T-bones marinating and maybe start a salad."

"Why?" asked Race. "Is Megan coming?"

"No. She was going to, but her father got sick."

"Well," reasoned Race, "if it's just us men, we don't have to eat salad if we don't want to. Do we?"

Eric considered that and nodded approval. "Good point. I must be mad. We'll have steak and baked potatoes loaded with sour cream, butter and bacon. I'll even throw a few chicken wings in the oven. We'll scarf down enough fat and salt to give Ghandi a heart attack."

Race lifted his beer, surprised by how calm and reassured he suddenly felt. It was good to be with friends, he thought, and to know that Candra was being looked after by someone who was young and strong, and trained to do it well. He toasted the air. "To red meat, fat and salt."

Eric clinked his bottle against Race's. "All we need is a good sports channel and we've got paradise."

Race was still chuckling when Eric disappeared through the patio doors into the kitchen.

* * * * *

Candra stepped into Drew's office and closed the door firmly behind her. She walked to the chair facing his desk and sat down. She clasped her hands in her lap and prepared for the worst. "Okay. Tell me. What did you find out?"

Drew tapped his fingers on his blotter. "Well, that's sweet. No hug? Not even a 'hi Drew, how're you doing?'"

She shifted in her chair and crossed her legs. Despite Drew's earlier assurances, visions of Race being led away in shackles crowded her vision and the words "first-degree murder" thrummed in her ears. Drew had figured it out. It was the only logical explanation for his urgent need to see her. What she couldn't figure out was why he hadn't posted a guard at the house to make sure his new suspect didn't make a run for it.

"I'm just not in the mood for niceties, I guess. It's bad news and I'd like to get it over with."

He nodded and pushed back his chair. He stood and reached for a file that lay closed neatly on his desk. Rounding the desk he hitched a hip on the corner and offered her the folder.

She accepted it gingerly and laid it open on her lap. "What's this?"

"It's the DNA report from the murder scene."

"DNA? You analyzed the DNA from the killer and the victim, right?"

"Yes. And Race. And it was through that analysis that we were able to definitively clear Race of any involvement in the attack."

She nodded, relaxed a little. "Right. But that's the good news. Why the big drama scene? I don't get it."

"Open the file."

Confused, she complied. She flipped through a few pages, took note of the names at the top of each page. "Okay, so you've got a report on the killer's DNA, the victim's and Race's."

"Right. The information exonerated Race but brought to light some new and rather disturbing...developments."

She looked down at the pages and shrugged, feeling frustrated. "Don't play with me, Drew. You know this is all gibberish to me. What am I missing?"

"Turn to the last page. The overall analysis."

She flipped over a few more sheets and came to the page he was speaking of.

"Read the conclusion at the bottom of the page," he instructed.

She found the paragraph and read it silently to herself. And then she read it again. Her breath suddenly burning in her lungs, she looked up at Drew in disbelief. "That can't be right. How can this possibly *be*?"

"I don't know, Candra, but I do know one thing. I don't believe in coincidences and I don't believe in accidents. I have a feeling you know more about how Race came to be at that cemetery that night than what you're telling me. And I think it's time I know everything you know."

"I can't, Drew," she breathed, staring at the words that could tear Race's fragile world apart. Race had trusted her and she couldn't betray that. Not even for a good friend like Drew. This meant nothing, after all. Didn't it? "I just can't."

Drew slid off the desk and knelt in front of her. He placed a hand gently over hers. "You're positive I can't change your mind?"

She nodded, feeling the burn of tears collecting behind her eyes. "I'm sorry, Drew, but I'm positive."

He stood. "All right, then. Let's go."

Startled, she looked up at him. "Go? Go where?"

"To see him. If you won't tell me what I need to know, then maybe he will. I had a meeting scheduled this afternoon, but now it's been canceled, so there's no reason not to do it now."

She leapt from the chair, sending the papers scattering across the floor. "You can't tell him this! You have no idea what it will do to him. If you tell him this…this…monster is his *father*, that he carries the blood of a killer in his veins, it…" She whirled away and stalked to the window, leaning her hot forehead against the cool glass. "It will destroy him."

She felt Drew move up behind her and lay a hand on her shoulder. "He has to know, Candra. Sooner or later, he has to know. And I need to know what this connection means to my case."

She said nothing, wished there was some way she could protect Race from yet another gruesome truth.

"And for his good, as well as the good of any future victims of that *monster*, I think the sooner he knows the better."

Candra looked at her watch and noted that it read 3:45. She was safe and she was miles away from sand or water. But suddenly she needed to be close to Race, and she suspected he needed to be close to her as well. "All right. Fine. Let's go."

"You're not going to fight me on this?"

She strode toward the door. "I only fight battles I know I can win." She tossed him a glance over her shoulder. "And besides, if I don't let you win once in a while, you'll stop playing with me."

He walked past her, grabbing her arm and dragging her along as he went. "If I didn't think you'd enjoy it, I'd take you over my knee for that."

"Promises, promises," she chuckled, but thoughts of Race and what she had to tell him never left her mind.

* * * * *

Eric finished ladling marinade over the steaks and carried the dish to the fridge. The steaks safely ensconced in their bed of sauce and spices, he picked up his beer and returned to the counter where he'd assembled tortilla chips, salsa, canned chili and spicy cheese sauce. He'd make a plate of nachos for them to snack on and maybe if it was spicy enough he'd actually manage to put a little color back in Race's cheeks.

He glanced out at the patio where Race lay, exactly where Eric had left him over an hour ago. Eric was pretty sure he'd fallen asleep—again. He wasn't buying the "flu" story. Not only did Race rarely get sick, but he never admitted weakness. There was something else going on here, and Eric was convinced it was something a lot more significant than some stray virus.

But since no one seemed inclined to fill him in on anything, he'd have to satisfy himself with pumping his friend full of calories and perhaps getting his adrenaline pumped up by watching a few good touchdowns.

He had just finished arranging the chips on the tray and was licking chili off his fingers when the front doorbell rang. "Candra?" he whispered to himself. "Could she be back already?" With a glance at his watch and a noncommittal shrug he washed his hands and trekked off toward the front of the house.

He glanced through the peephole and wasn't overly surprised to see a man in a courier uniform. He preferred to get parcels delivered to the office, but occasionally business associates took liberties and sent documents or packages to his home.

Smiling and already reaching for the clipboard to sign his name, he opened the door.

The bullet slammed into him with so much force it hurled him backward, sending him sprawling. He hit the floor hard, slid across the polished marble, finally coming to rest with his head against the base of the table in the center of the hall. He stared at the ceiling struggling for breath and battling a pain he'd never dreamed possible. He only caught a fleeting image of a figure standing over him before his attacker walked away, leaving Eric to die alone.

* * * * *

Not bothering to open his eyes, Race reached for the beer bottle he'd left sitting on the patio beside him. He placed it to his lips and tipped it up, but was rewarded with only a paltry few drops of lukewarm liquid.

"Damn," he muttered, setting the bottle back on the stones. "Where the hell is Eric, anyway? Some host he is."

"Eric is somewhat…indisposed."

At the sound of the strange voice, Race's eyes flew open. He barely had time to register the report of the pistol before the pain flared in his shoulder. He saw the face of the man standing at the foot of his deck chair and the terror struck surprisingly hard and deep—just before the world went black.

Chapter Fifteen

සැ

Race became aware of the sound of the waves first. The soft hiss and sigh of water as it lapped against the beach. He heard the distant cry of seagulls, felt the warmth of the sun on his face, and sand between his fingertips.

And then he realized his wrists were bound together and his eyes flew open, but he had to blink furiously against the bright sunlight.

"Ah," rasped a familiar male voice. "He's awake. Considering how quick that stuff works, I'd have thought you'd be out for hours."

At last his tormentor came into view. He stepped close to Race and crouched down in the sand. Race caught the glint of metal first—the evil gleam of a wicked hunting knife clutched tightly in the man's hand. Then he lifted his eyes, met the other's gaze—and his breath caught in his throat.

Tall and lanky, with blade-like cheekbones and eyes as flat and black as hunks of cast iron, Race recognized him immediately.

He was the man from the motel room, and from the cemetery. He was the one who had eluded Race's efforts and tossed his world into chaos. He continued to hold Race's gaze, studying him like a spider scrutinizing a fly in its web. Just as before, his gaze paralyzed Race, his mere presence seemed to have the ability to suck the energy from Race's body.

"What is it, by the way? What do you put in those things?"

Race blinked, startled by the question. "What? What things?"

"Those dart things I found at your little hideout." His thin lips parted in a mocking grin. "I followed the cops there, but they didn't quite get everything. Lucky for me."

Race blinked, trying to assimilate what he was hearing. "You were at my place? Why?"

"Because I needed to know." Then he bent very low, low enough that Race could smell his breath laced with cigarette smoke and rancor. "Who the hell *are* you, boy? Why do you keep—"

Race's fists, bound together by cord, slammed into his jaw with so much force that he could hear the man's teeth crack together. His head snapped backward and his ass hit the ground with a resounding thump.

Realizing too late that his feet were bound as well as his fists, Race scrambled backward across the sand, trying desperately to put some distance between himself and his captor. He rolled onto his stomach and had just managed to draw up his knees when a foot slammed into his ribs, hurling him back to the sand and sending pain shooting through his side.

On his back, and struggling for breath, he looked up at the man's face, contorted in rage. "You idiot." He placed the cold edge of the blade against Race's cheekbone. "You think you have a hope in hell of getting out of here?" As he spoke, he drew a thin line with the blade across Race's cheek. He felt no pain, only the warmth of blood as it trickled down his skin. "You think there's any fucking way you're going to make it out of this room alive?"

Room? Race's gaze flitted to his surroundings and at last he realized the truth. He wasn't on a beach, or beside an ocean. He wasn't even outdoors. He was in Eric's tropical fantasy room in the basement of his mansion.

Eric! Fuck! "Where is he?" His throat felt like it was full of gravel. "Where's Eric?"

"We're not here to talk about your fucking friends, *Race*." Sneering, he leaned back and wiped the blade clean on his shirt. "We're here to talk about you and how it is that you keep popping up in my life like a bad rash!"

Race lay back his head and closed his eyes. The cut began to throb but he barely noticed the pain. He was thinking of Eric and hoping against hope that he had gotten away, and thanking the gods that somehow it was him on this beach, facing a killer rather than Candra. He didn't know how he could have gotten that confused, but then again, the vision had been strange, disjointed and foggy, not like his usual experiences at all. He'd just had this sense that it was someone he cared about and knew well, and since the victims were always women, he'd deduced it had to be Candra.

He'd never dreamed he'd been viewing his own death scene.

A fitting irony, he thought, but one he could have done without.

"Hey!" Knuckles crashed against Race's jaw. "I'm talking to you."

Race's head snapped to the side and he felt a fresh trickle of blood on his lip, but didn't open his eyes.

"What the hell kind of name is that, anyway? What bitch-whore mother would name her kid after a goddamn *sport*?"

At mention of his mother, Race's eyes flew open.

"Ah *ha*!" laughed the man. "That got a rise outta you. You a momma's boy, then, are you? Don't like it when somebody calls your mommy names? But then again maybe it's a sen-si-tive topic 'cause she gets called that a lot. Maybe your momma likes to spread her legs for anything with a dick and a twenty in his pants."

Hands bunched into fists, Race launched himself from the sand, but he was too weak and the man too fast. He dodged the attack and managed to land a solid elbow to Race's ribs as he passed by. Race landed in the sand once again, writhing in pain even as he struggled to get to his knees.

"See?" taunted the man, pushing Race over easily and looming over him. "Just like I said, sen-si-tive. Where's your momma now, anyway? Maybe I could find her and she could join our little party. It would make up for losing that sweet little piece of ass that took off on you this afternoon. I had plans for her, but when that cop came and took her away I decided I'd have to make that sacrifice so I could get a crack at you. This big old, isolated mausoleum fit my plans to a T."

He grinned again, the effect grisly. "So what do you say? We'll call up your mom and invite her to the party. You could watch me fuck her to death and then cut off little pieces of her to feed to you." He lifted the knife and examined it lovingly. "What do you think of that?"

"I think you're a sick, twisted son of a bitch who's not fit to walk the face of the planet, let alone lick the ground my mother walked on!"

He laughed again, apparently feeding off Race's wrath. "So she's a saint then, eh? A regular fucking *nun*? But then again, those are the best kind—the ones who want you to think they're Miss Purity. They say they don't want it but are really just itchin' for ya to tie 'em down and fuck 'em in the ass until they beg for more." He batted his eyelashes and raised his voice in a hideous parody of a woman. "Oh, Anton, baby. Harder. Fuck me *harder*."

The heat that had begun to bubble in Race's veins suddenly turned to ice. *Anton*. That name. There was something about that name…

*****

"Fucking bitch!" The slap of flesh against bone rang in Race's ears. His mother's head snapped to the side and her blood sprayed across the bedcovers. "You thought you could hide from me? Did you actually think I wouldn't find you?" He grabbed her by the shoulders and dragged her up off the bed, forcing her to look at him. "Did you?"

The sight of the blood dribbling down her chin had Race's hands fisted into tiny knots of rage. But he stayed put. He'd promised.

"I…I'm sorry, Anton."

"I'm sorry, Anton?" he mimicked, shaking her. "That's all you've got? I invested money in you, dammit! I bought you clothes, I sent you to a fuckin' salon. I made you into something men would crawl across broken glass for, and this is the thanks I get? Running away and hiding from me?"

"I've got some money, if you want it." She raised her hand to point at the door. "In the other room. If we could just go in my—"

He threw her back onto the bed and ripped open her blouse. "Oh, I'll get my money all right, but first…" He pulled a knife out of a sheath on his calf and quickly cut away her skirt and panties. "Anton DuGuay will exact payment his way…"

Race fell back into the present like a man hitting the ground without a parachute. He couldn't breathe, could barely see for the emotions that surged through him.

Rage, grief and anguish combined to form a tornado that twisted through his soul. His eyes flew open and when he saw Anton's face he accepted the truth. This was the man who had tortured and murdered his mother. The man who had raped her and cut off her breasts. The man who had hacked up Race's world and decimated his future as surely as he'd mutilated his mother. The one emotion lacking from the whirlwind, however was fear. Fear had been displaced by righteousness, exhaustion by empowerment. This was the moment he'd been waiting for his whole life, and he had no intention of allowing anything as insignificant as a knife or a few pieces of nylon cord to keep him from achieving his goal—he glanced at the man who stood over him—the bloody, torturous death of Anton Duguay.

* * * * *

Candra felt a vast sense of relief as they pulled into Eric's drive and eased to a stop by the front door. It had felt wrong to be separated from Race while he was still so weak and vulnerable, and she was glad that she'd soon be close to him again.

But as she took Drew's hand and allowed him to draw her out of the car and lead her up the steps, the heaviness returned.

"What's wrong?" asked Drew, apparently sensing her distress. "Suddenly you look so pale."

"I don't know, Drew. I just don't know how I can face this. It'll kill him. I just know it."

Drew reached for the bell. "He's stronger than you give him credit for."

She just shook her head. Drew didn't know the full extent of Race's vulnerabilities, and at that moment she accepted that he could never know. No matter how much she hated keeping things from Drew she accepted that she could never share what she knew of Race's history with him. Drew was a cop first, and his duty would be clear. She had to keep it from him for all their sakes.

Drew rang the bell and the chimes echoed through the house. They waited several minutes and when there was no response Candra grabbed his sleeve. "Let's go around back. They're probably at the pool."

But Drew hesitated. "Hang on. The door's open."

"What?" Upon closer inspection she realized he was right. The door was open a crack, and when Drew nudged it with his foot, it swung in freely. They stepped into the elaborate foyer, and Candra let out a shriek of horror. "Eric!"

They rushed across the polished marble floor and sank to their knees beside him. Eric lay in a pool of his own blood which continued to leak from a wound in his chest. His eyes were open, however, and he seemed to focus on Candra.

"Eric," she cried even as she ripped off her T-shirt and pressed it to the wound. "Oh my God. Who did this?" She could hear Drew, already shouting instructions into his cell phone.

Eric's lips moved but no sound came out. He was struggling to breathe, his chest heaving as if weighed down by a thousand-pound sack of sand.

"I think his lung is punctured," said Drew, slipping the cell phone back into his pocket. "You keep pressing on the wound and I'll be right back."

"Be right back?" she wailed. "Where are you going?" But Drew had already disappeared.

She turned her attention back to Eric whose hand had latched around her wrist and was squeezing with surprising strength. His lips moved and she thought, perhaps he was forming the word "Race".

Terror speared through her. "Race? Oh God. What happened? Where is he?"

But at that moment Drew reappeared with, of all things, a roll of plastic wrap. "What the hell?" she asked.

"It's called an occlusive dressing. It'll help plug the hole and let him breathe easier. Now help me lift him."

They spent the next minute wrapping the film around Eric's torso and suffering through his moans of pain, but when they finished she realized Drew had been right. Eric's breathing had eased and he closed his eyes in apparent relief.

The blood, however, continued to pool around him. It now stained both her and Drew's clothes. Drew removed his jacket and draped it over Eric to help ward off shock.

"Eric," pleaded Candra. "Do you know where Race is? Is he alive?"

Eric's eyes opened, but it was obvious it was an effort. He said nothing, but lifted his hand and pointed.

She followed his gaze and whispered, "Oh God."

"What?" asked Drew. "What's in there?"

"That alcove leads to the basement."

"The basement? What the hell's in the basement?"

She jumped to her feet. "Apparently Race is. And I have to go down there."

Drew grabbed her hand before she could get far. "Oh no, you don't. If he's down there, he's down there with someone very dangerous, and no way in hell I'm letting you go."

"You have to stay with Eric until the ambulance comes."

"No." He pulled her back, and motioned for her to sit. "You do."

"But—"

"No buts." He pulled his gun out of its holster and flipped off the safety. "You stay, and send down backup when they get here."

She grabbed his shirt and hung on tight as she whispered, "Please, Drew. I love him."

He touched her cheek. "I know you do, Candy-bar."

And then he was gone.

* * * * *

Race turned his face away from Anton and closed his eyes, allowing his body to go limp and forcing his fists to unclench.

"Is that it?" ranted Anton. "I talk about fucking your mother's ass and you got nothing to say?"

His lips brushing against the sand, Race murmured something unintelligible.

"Huh?" Anton stepped closer, kicked Race in the ribs. "What did you say?"

Race's groan of pain was sincere and it convinced him that he had at least one or two cracked ribs. But when he rolled onto his stomach and tried to draw up his knees and pull himself to all fours, the lethargy of his movements was feigned.

Another blow from Anton's boot sent Race flying. The force of slamming against the wall of the fantasy room was enough to knock the breath out of him and to give his neck a jolt when his head hit the drywall.

He groaned again, and allowed his head to loll, but remained alert to Anton's movements.

The toe of Anton's boot nudged his side. "Answer me, or there'll be lots more where that came from."

"What?" said Race, lacing his voice with as much desperation and fear as he could muster. "What do you want from me?"

Anton chuckled. "Oh, I want a lot of things. I want you screaming in pain and begging for mercy. I want your throat gaping open and your blood on my clothes. But all that in due time." He crouched down and whispered, "At the moment weak and pathetic will do just fine, *and* I want to know what you said a minute ago. You know…about your bitch-whore mother."

Race's whisper was barely audible. "I said, she's dead."

Sheathing his knife, Anton grabbed Race's shirt and hauled him to his feet. He slammed Race against the wall. "What?" he yelled.

Race allowed his head to loll forward, forced himself to remain limp, lifeless. Seemingly helpless.

"Dammit!" raged Anton, shaking him. "Speak up before I beat it out of you."

Race swallowed thickly, made an exaggerated effort to lift his head and moisten his lips. His eyes fluttered open. "I…I said…" He licked his lips again.

"Oh, for chrissake." His hands still embedded in Race's shirt, Anton leaned in closer, close enough that Race could smell his rancid breath. "Tell me or I'll rip out your fucking tongue and beat you with it."

Race lifted his head and blinked slowly, as if trying to focus on Anton's face. Odd, he thought in that moment, that the man's gaze had now lost its power over him. It was as if the realization of Anton's identity had severed whatever nebulous bond had held them together.

He swallowed. "I said…" In the next instant every muscle in Race's body zinged to red alert. With his bound hands, he grabbed Anton's shirt and dragged him closer, close enough that Race could reach his face with his mouth.

Before Anton could come to his senses and realize what was happening, Race had sunk his teeth into Anton's lower lip. He bit down like a man tearing into a hunk of rare steak. He bit and held, pushing Anton's body away, even as his teeth clicked together, tearing through skin and severing flesh.

Anton stumbled backward, screaming and clutching at his mouth that was already spurting blood and drool like a macabre fountain.

Race dove forward, knocking Anton to the floor and landing on top of him. He pulled the knife from its sheath even as he spat the vile piece of flesh into a pile of sand.

"You bastard!" screamed Anton, writhing on the sand, scrambling frantically for some shred of sanity in his world of pain and panic. "You goddamn fucking bastard!"

Race rolled away and quickly cut through the cords that bound his feet. He then held the knife in his teeth to work at the cord around his wrists.

At that moment Anton ceased his struggles and seemed to become aware of what was happening. Momentarily forgetting his mutilated face, he focused on Race, let out a bloodcurdling scream and surged to his feet, running full tilt toward Race.

He was greeted with a solid kick to his solar plexus that sent him reeling backward and left him gagging and heaving yet more blood and bile into the sand. It took Race less than ten seconds to cut through the last of the cord and free himself of all handicaps.

The knife clutched firmly in his hand, he strode over to Anton, grabbed him by his bloodstained shirt and hauled him to his feet. He quickly disarmed Anton of the gun tucked snugly in the back of his jeans. "Forget about this?" he asked with a sardonic grin. "Funny how panic and agonizing pain can do that to you." He stuffed the gun in the back of his own jeans before backhanding Anton across the cheek and throwing him away like a rotten piece of fruit. He was rewarded with a satisfying *thunk* as Anton's head hit the drywall and he slid to the ground, babbling incoherently and clutching once again at his absent lip.

"That one was for me," said Race, his voice low and deadly. He strode over to Anton and towered over him. Feeling empowered — like the god of justice — he examined the blade, enjoying the way it glinted in the harsh artificial sunlight. "What comes next, however, will be for Mom."

* * * * *

Drew pushed open another door and burst into the room. Shouting his warning, he went in low with gun drawn and trigger ready. He found the room devoid of occupants, but yet again, his surroundings stunned and astonished him. He found himself in a dank, dark jungle. The air was heavy with moisture, the room replete with ferns and low-hanging branches. The ground was spongy beneath his feet, and he could hear the distant gurgle of water. A leopard roared behind him, the effect so realistic he jumped at the noise.

He had to force himself to refocus on his task. He made a good thorough sweep of the room and confirmed once again that it was unoccupied before slipping out into the hall and closing the door behind him.

He mopped his brow and allowed himself a moment to regroup. Race was in danger but Drew wouldn't be much help to either of them if he wasn't thinking rationally. And at the moment, it was difficult to maintain his perspective considering the disturbing information that was coming to light about Megan's boss and so-called friend.

Drew shook that off and headed to the next door. He'd checked three rooms so far, and judging from the gargoyles that lined the hall, three remained.

He headed to the next door and found a mermaid adorning its façade. He quietly checked the latch and, once again, found it unlocked. The door at the top of the stairs had been equipped with an elaborate brass lock, but it had been no match for a couple of .38 caliber bullets. Anton had blown his way through the main door, but the doors to the individual rooms had no locks. Apparently Eric hadn't felt the need to protect the rest of his…paraphernalia.

Drew shuddered slightly, even as he pressed his ear to the wood and listened. He heard nothing, but guessed that it was a futile exercise anyway, as the rooms were likely soundproofed. He'd have to go in blind, just as before.

He placed his hand on the latch, readied his weapon, took a deep breath and burst inside.

"Police!" he yelled. "Drop your weapon!" His arms outstretched and finger tight on the trigger, he blinked in surprise. "Race?"

Race, standing in the center of the room, about fifteen feet away, whirled at the sound of Drew's voice. Shirtless and streaked with blood, his appearance was startling. But upon closer scrutiny Drew decided that at least some of the blood had come from the other occupant of the room.

The man lay directly behind Race, bound to what appeared to be an old wooden raft. The rough-hewn look was a deception, however. The "raft" was actually nothing of the sort. It boasted a variety of straps and pads and Drew could make out hinges and mechanisms that had purposes he could barely dream of. The apparatus had been raised up and tilted on a forty-five degree angle to allow Race access to his captive.

Drew dragged his attention back to Race — back to the man who had now produced a gun and trained it on Drew.

"Get out, Drew," said Race, his voice surprisingly calm considering the sweat that gleamed on his skin and the fire that burned in his eyes. Blood also dripped slowly from a wound on his cheek. "I have unfinished business here."

Drew held his ground. "You know I can't do that, Race. Put down the gun and let's talk about this."

Race shook his head slowly, almost sadly. "You can forget the canned hostage negotiation lines. They're tired and meaningless and besides, there's nothing to talk about. This is the man who killed my mother, and he has to pay for that. He *will* pay for that. There's no room for discussion."

Drew blinked stupidly, assimilating this new information. He also had little doubt that this was the man whose DNA matched Race's so closely. And then, of course, he realized how perfectly the pieces fit together.

Race's mother had fled her pimp when she'd realized she was pregnant with his child. She'd no doubt felt that escape was the only way to save herself and her child from a man whose violent tendencies had no doubt been all too apparent.

The fact that the pimp had eventually found and murdered his errant employee was easy enough to believe — a common story among those who dabbled in the sex trade. But that Race and his father had crossed paths again? *That* was the coincidence that Drew found hard to swallow. He didn't believe in coincidences, but at the moment had no other explanation for it.

All of that flitted through his mind in a moment.

"He will pay, Race. But you have to let the system exact that payment."

"The system?" Race's laughter skittered across Drew's skin like a thousand tiny needles. "The system can't tell its ass from a hole in the ozone. *Fuck* the system! This is *my* battle, Drew, my pain, and my vengeance. I've been owed this moment for twenty-five fucking years, and I intend to enjoy it."

Drew's heart was pounding in his chest like a freight train. The compassionate man inside him warred with the cop, but there was little doubt as to the outcome. "You know I can't let you do that. I can't let you harm that man, and I can't let you throw your own life away."

"Life?" yelled Race. "What life? I'm not living a life! I'm living a fucking *nightmare*!"

Suddenly shouts and yells and the sound of pounding feet filled the air. Three more police officers tumbled into the room, all shouting warnings and instructions, all with guns drawn and aimed directly at the threat. All aimed at Race.

Race's instincts kicked in and he reacted in a heartbeat. Before any shots could be fired he had rounded the raft, placing Anton between himself and the police, and placing the gun to Anton's temple.

Anton struggled against his bindings but the effort was weak. He'd already lost a fair bit of blood from his lip, as well as taken a sound beating. Race had wanted him weak and docile in order to facilitate his being bound to the raft, and what was to come afterward.

The beating had been a disappointment. Race had been surprised by how little satisfaction he'd gleaned from the process, but he was certain that the more intense *experiences* he had in mind for Anton would live up to expectations.

But now Drew and this handful of misguided officers were trying to come between him and his destiny. They couldn't understand how important this was — how essential. He couldn't step away from it. There was no way in hell.

"Get out!" he screamed. "Don't you understand? He's a monster. He *needs* to die. Let me finish this!"

"Jesus, Race," said Drew. "If you don't drop that fucking gun, you know full well there's only one way this is going to finish." He adjusted his grip on his weapon and Race could see the sweat beading on his forehead. "And I don't want to be the one zipping you into a goddamn body bag!"

"Fuck," muttered Race to himself, fighting the pressure that had begun to build in his chest. It wasn't supposed to be like this. "Fuck, fuck, fuck." And then more loudly. "I can't. I can't let him go. Don't ask me to let him go." His voice was shaking and he hated himself for that.

"Please, Race. Please let him go. For me."

The sound of Candra's voice slammed into him like a bullet. "Candra?" he rasped.

But it was Drew who voiced his thoughts. "For God's sake, Candra. Get out of here."

But she didn't listen. In fact she stepped further into the room, only to be dragged back by one of the officers.

"Get your hands off her," yelled Race, "or I'll shoot him right now!" He cocked the trigger to drive home the threat, and was rewarded with a pathetic moan of terror from his mother's killer.

"Let her go," ordered Drew.

They let her go and Race relaxed. "Get out, Candra. Please."

She shook her head slowly, tried to smile. "Race, when have you ever known me to do what you tell me to do?"

He wanted to laugh, but his soul was twisted in knots. He couldn't put her in danger. But he couldn't let go of this either. He felt like he was being ripped in two.

And he had no idea how to put himself back together.

Candra felt as if her heart was crumbling inside her chest.

The agony on Race's face cut through her as surely as a blade piercing her body. She wanted to help him—needed to help him in a way so deep and intense, she could barely comprehend it. But at that moment she wasn't sure how, and she just prayed that her uncertainty wouldn't end up getting him killed. She decided to go with her heart.

"I can't go, Race. Surely you know that. I'm in this with you—no matter what."

Sweat trickled down his cheek and she saw him adjust his grip on the gun, press it more firmly against Anton's temple. "No, you're not. This has nothing to do with you. This is my fight, babe. Mine alone. Thinking that you could help me with it was an illusion."

"No, it wasn't, dammit!" She tried to step closer but was stopped by Drew's outstretched arm. The warning in his eyes was clear. She could stay and play negotiator, try to keep Race from getting Anton, as well as himself killed, but she would not be allowed to step into the line of fire.

She took a deep breath and said more calmly, "No, it wasn't. You said your life was a nightmare, Race, and I understand that. It has been. It's been painful and horrible and…" She struggled for words that were inadequate. "It's been something that I know I can never begin to understand."

He nodded agreement.

"But you were almost out of the nightmare. You're just one small step away from leaving all that behind, Race. All you have to do is take it. Take that step."

"Oh? And what step is that? Letting my mother's killer go *free*?"

"Yes."

He laughed. "Fuck that, Candra. Fuck *that*!"

"You have to let go of the guilt and the anger, Race. That's what's tied you to the nightmare all these years. That's what has kept you in the dark. You have to let go of all that and embrace what's good in your life. Let yourself enjoy it."

A tear trickled down his cheek. "What goodness? Tell me, Candra. Tell me what's left. What is there to embrace?"

"There's friendship. You have friends who care about you. Friends like Eric and Megan—"

"Eric? Eric's dead."

"No. No he's not. He's on his way to the hospital and he's hurt, but they're pretty sure he'll make it."

He blinked, obviously shocked by the news and trying to accept it.

"And there's me. I love you, Race. I'm sorry I didn't say it sooner, but it's true. I love you and I need you, and dammit I can help you step out of the nightmare if you just take my hand and let me."

He met her gaze, held it. "Don't love me, Candra. People who love me get hurt. They die."

"That's melodramatic bullshit, and you know it. Loving you doesn't put anyone in danger. I'm not going to die, and neither are you, if you just put down that damn gun and step away from him. Let go of it. Let go of all of it. You just have to let go and allow yourself to be happy." She wished so desperately to be able to touch him. "Killing him isn't going to free you of the guilt, it'll only *add* to it. Forgive yourself. Let yourself be loved and you'll be free of the nightmare."

He licked his lips, stared at her. And then he shifted his gaze to his victim, and she knew he was weakening.

"He can't get away with it." His voice had taken on a haunting edge, a "lost-boy" quality. "He's hurt too many people. He can't get away unpunished."

"Don't worry," said Drew. "I give you my word. He's going to suffer in prison and feel a lot more pain for a lot longer than what you could have inflicted here, today."

"You can assure me of that?"

"I swear on my badge."

Race met Candra's gaze again, took a deep breath. Nodded slowly. "All right."

"Okay then," said Drew cautiously. "Let's do this by the book. Put down the gun. Very slowly. And then put your hands on your head."

It was hard to watch. It was hard to see him submit to the police, to see the handcuffs go on and be frisked like a criminal. But it was necessary, she knew. And when they finally let her through and her arms latched around his neck and she felt the warmth of his flesh against hers, and the steady beat of his heart against her own, she knew it was all worth it.

Out of the corner of her eye, she saw the officers release Anton from his bindings and move him to a stretcher. He didn't struggle at all, having apparently succumbed to shock and fallen into unconsciousness.

She turned her attention back to what was important—back to Race. His hands cuffed behind his back, he was unable to hug her back, but he nuzzled her throat. "You're crazy, you know. Bursting into a room full of cops and guns like you know no fear."

She pulled away and cupped his jaw in her hands. "Are you kidding? I did it because I *was* afraid, Race. I was terrified—terrified of losing you." And now the relief was shaded by a new fear. "But before they take you away, there's something I need to tell you. I hate to do it, but I don't think I have the right to keep it from you any longer."

He tilted his head, the confusion in his eyes plain. "Oh? What is it?"

But she didn't get a chance to answer.

An ear-piercing scream cut through the somber mood, and suddenly gunfire filled the air.

She heard, "You fucking son of a bitch!" an instant before Race's body jerked and his face registered surprise. He toppled forward and fell soundlessly at her feet.

She collapsed beside him, screaming his name, and only vaguely aware of Anton's body spasming in death as it was riddled with bullets from three police officers' guns.

Chapter Sixteen

Two weeks later

ೲ

Candra strolled along the beach, her feet splashing through the warm, shallow waves, her eyes scanning the horizon. The late afternoon sun had begun to set, bleeding vivid golds and purples across the sky and into the water. She could smell the tang of the ocean and the subtle sweetness of the seagrass and wildflowers that dotted the shoreline.

She paused for a moment, allowing her feet to sink into the wet sand as she considered the beauty and vastness around her. She'd been reminding herself to take such moments, lately. To take time to enjoy the small joys that life afforded her. If there was one thing the last few weeks had taught her, it was to enjoy what the world offered, *when* it was offered.

She turned, glanced back toward the cabin, and a smile broke across her lips. "Race?" she whispered to herself. "What the hell are you up to?"

She resumed her trek, picking up the pace to speed her return to the cabin.

"Finally," grumbled Race when she arrived and stood, glaring at him sitting on his blanket. "What the hell took you so long?"

She shook her head in wonder. "Race Kendall, when I left you, you were lounging in bed, nibbling on barbecue potato chips, watching *Casablanca* and nursing that shoulder of yours."

"I was playing possum," he said with a kind of mischievous grin that she didn't think she'd ever seen on his lips before. "I seem to be rather good at it."

As was your father, she thought, but kept it to herself. Anton's "possum" act had not only allowed him to reach for a police officer's gun and hence lead to his own death, but it had also resulted in yet another injury for Race.

The shoulder wound had been superficial, but his weakened state, combined with all the other stresses in his life, had been enough to convince Candra that it was best to keep her secret a little while longer. With Anton dead there was no rush to fill Race in on his connection to the killer. She knew she'd have to tell him eventually, but decided to wait until he was stronger, both physically and emotionally.

But now, judging from the crackling fire, the blanket, the basket filled with wine, cheese and fresh bread, and Race's blistering smile, she decided that he was as recovered as he was going to get. And that knowledge filled her with dread.

"Hey!" He reached for her hand and drew her down onto the blanket. "What's wrong? Suddenly you look so sad. Did I forget something?"

She shook her head. "No. Everything's perfect. It's been a long time since I had a picnic on the beach."

He brushed a finger along her jaw. "Then why the long face? This was supposed to make you glow with happiness, not wither with disappointment."

She grasped his wrist and pressed his hand more firmly to her cheek. "I'm not disappointed. I'm very happy."

"But?"

She sighed, releasing his hand. "But I have something to tell you. I've been putting it off, waiting until you were strong enough to handle it..."

He leaned back on the blanket, propped himself up on his elbows. His smile faded as he studied her. "Okay, so I guess I'm strong enough now. What is it?"

She studied him, biting her lower lip, still uncertain.

He laughed and reached for her hand. "Come on, Candra. What is it? Whatever it is, it can't be that bad."

"It's about Anton."

He nodded, maintaining the smile although she knew it was forced. "Yeah? What about him?"

"You're making progress," she laughed. "That's the first time I've heard you refer to him without using profanity."

"Candra…"

"Sorry." She swallowed, took a deep breath. "It was what Drew wanted to talk to me about that day. It concerns the DNA evidence that they gathered from you and Anton."

Race stared at her, and said very slowly, "He was my father."

She gaped in astonishment. "What? But…how—"

"That's it, isn't it?"

"Yes! But how could you possibly know?"

He let out a soft chuckle and flopped back on the blanket, staring up at the color-scarred sky.

She joined him, draping herself over him and resting her head on his chest so that she could hear and feel the reassuring beat of his heart. She waited for him to speak.

"I think…I guess I always knew. Now that I think about it…it only makes sense. I can't believe I didn't realize it sooner."

She nuzzled the soft cotton of his shirt. "I'm sorry, Race. You've had enough nasty surprises in your life. I'm sorry that you have to deal with yet one more."

"No." He stroked her back. "It's all right. It explains a lot, and in a way...it helps it all make sense."

"It all?"

"The visions, the guilt, my inability to let go of my mother's pain, and my need to feel other victims' pain. All of that. Or none of it. I don't know. Maybe in the grand scheme of things I was being asked to make up for my father's sins, and now that he's gone and I've lost my link to the victims, I can finally move on."

It had only been a few weeks, but he'd told her he felt different, more complete. As if a door somewhere deep inside had closed. He was certain that his powers of foresight had died along with his father.

He shrugged, wrapped his arms around her and squeezed. "It doesn't matter anymore. If you had told me that a month ago it would have devastated me. But now..."

She lifted her head and smiled down at him. "I think you're whole again, Race Kendall. I think you found all the pieces of you that were missing."

Suddenly he grabbed her and rolled over, pinning her beneath him and securing her with a kiss. His mouth was soft but insistent, his lips gentle but possessive. His tongue traced her teeth and his hands skimmed her hair.

When he finally lifted his head and looked at her, his gaze held the old fire, the same intensity and passion that had drawn her to him that first day in Eric's study.

"You were the biggest part of that, Candra. You were what was missing."

She smiled, trying to make light of what he was saying and ignore the frantic pounding in her chest. "Are you saying what I think you're saying?"

"If you think I'm saying I love you, then you're right." He whisked a kiss across her cheek, traced his tongue around the curl of her ear. "You said it two weeks ago, but God knows I should have said it long before that because I knew it was the truth."

He moved on to her throat, his lips brushing her skin as he said, "I knew it, but didn't want to accept it."

She slid her hands up under his T-shirt. She never tired of touching him, of the smoothness of his skin or of the firm ridges of muscle that shifted and played beneath.

"And when did you know?" she asked, the shivers skittering down her arms as he toyed with her earlobe.

He whispered in her ear, "I knew the moment you took me up on that damn challenge." He lifted his head and smiled down at her. "I remember thinking, *Shit*! *What the hell have I gotten myself into?* You didn't back down, and I knew I was in deep — heart and soul."

She ran her fingers down his spine, pleased by the way his skin shivered at her touch, and thrilling to the way his growing erection now pressed against her cleft. "You know we haven't made love since the shooting."

"That's because you were babying me, feeding me soup and making me watch sappy movies." He slid a hand under her T-shirt and pushed aside the flimsy bikini top she wore beneath. He cupped a breast and tweaked a nipple. "It was like you were afraid I'd break."

She shuddered slightly. "You *were* broken, Race. For a long time…you were."

He suddenly sat up and grabbed her hands, dragged her to her feet, and whipped her T-shirt over her head. He tugged at the ties on her bikini top and it fell away as he reached for her shorts. "Hey!" she laughed. "What are you doing?"

"I'm not broken anymore. In fact I'm feeling stronger and more energetic than I have in years." Her shorts and bikini bottoms fell to her ankles. "And I feel like going skinny-dipping."

Before she could draw breath to point out that he still had a couple of layers of clothing on, he had shed every last stitch and stood before her, nude, his skin shimmering gold in the late afternoon sun.

"God," she breathed, skimming her hands over his chest. "Why do you have to be so damn beautiful?"

He growled. "Men aren't supposed to be beautiful. They're supposed to be virile, macho." He struck a pose. "*Manly.*"

She rolled her eyes, and on impulse, made a dash for the water. "Last one in is—" But he'd already hit the water, diving in and tossing up a wash of spray that soaked her skin and plastered her hair to her scalp.

She stood there, in water to her thighs and fumed. "That's not fair. You could have at least—" He burst out of the water just in front of her, grabbed her by the waist, picked her up and threw her in as easily as if he were tossing a reluctant puppy. She went under, took a couple of strokes to get her bearings, planted her feet on the bottom and launched herself out of the water, ready to do battle.

He snatched her out of midair and drew her close. His arms held her body like bands of steel, and his eyes danced with mischief. Plastered against him, and unable to do anything about it, she wrapped her legs around his hips.

His cock nudged her pussy and slid inside effortlessly.

She sucked in a breath and sighed, shifting so that he penetrated more deeply. He filled her, satisfied her and made her want all at the same time. "You don't play fair."

"Of course not," he said, walking out into the waves until they were chest-deep in warm, salty water. "I believe in getting what I want, and doing whatever it takes to get it."

"And you want me?"

"Mm-hmm." He held her hips and shifted his body, withdrawing from her and pumping deep again. She allowed her head to fall back in ecstasy and was pleased to feel his mouth on her breast. He circled her nipple with his tongue and murmured, "I've wanted you every day from the moment I saw you."

He covered her breast with his mouth and sucked hard. She lifted her head and watched him, watched the way the muscles in his jaw worked and the way his shoulders tensed at her touch.

Her pulse thrummed in her throat and her clit throbbed. It was as if every fiber of her being, every molecule had begun to buzz with awareness. The water lapping at her skin, the feel of his mouth on her breast, his hands on her hips, his cock inside her—the way his eyes hungered for her.

"I want you, too, Race," she breathed, plowing her fingers through his wet hair. "I want you, too."

He released her breast. "Touch yourself." His fingers dug more deeply into her hips. "I want to see you come."

She kissed him hard, dipping her tongue deep before drawing away and cupping her breasts with her hands. She massaged them, tweaked her nipples and savored the fire that leapt to his eyes as he watched.

He pumped harder. "Your clit. Touch your clit."

Using one hand to anchor herself to his shoulder, her other skimmed down her belly, beneath the surface of the water, and slipped between her thighs. Holding his gaze, she drew soft little circles over her swollen clit and savored the growing ache.

"Harder," he said. "Now."

She was startled to feel his finger slide insi͗
the added pressure almost sent her over the t͟ss, but
closed involuntarily as she sensed the approachin͗ eyes

"No." His voice, low and firm, was comman͟ʸes
vibrated in her chest. "Look at me."

She struggled to comply, the heaviness oʲ
making the effort Herculean.

"That's good," he said, pushing further inside ͟
pumping his cock inside her. "Now come."

And she did. With a cry of satisfaction she cam͓
pleasure pounding her like waves pounding the shore,
her contractions milking him to his own explosive climax.

He held her tight, his cock so deep she could feeʲ
nudge her womb as he pumped himself into her and allow͓
the waves to wash the heat and sweat from their skin.

Relaxed, but still holding her tight, he rested his
forehead on her shoulder. "You wear me out, Candra.
Nobody has ever worn me out like you."

She giggled. "I think that's probably the nicest
compliment you've ever paid me."

Still carrying her, he turned and walked back toward the
shore. Dripping and sated he set her down at the water's
edge and kneeled between her legs. "Lay back," he said.

She still felt a little dazed. "What?"

"You heard me. Lay back. I'm not done."

"Oh. Okay."

Giggling and drunk on her own happiness she lay back
on the sand and allowed him to touch and explore her pussy.
"What does it mean, by the way?" he asked, his fingers
rubbing her clit in slow, sweet circles.

"Uh. What? What does what mean?"

two fingers inside her, pumped slowly.

He in unusual and I've always wondered."

"Your na her lips, decided she didn't need to bother
Shes open anymore. "Candra means pure and

keepi
cha nd of his laughter she cracked open an eye.

ents had a knack for irony, Candra. I gotta give

may not be pure, but you sure chased me

the
and ly rolled his eyes and bent his head, and when
uched her clit she forgot completely what they
alking about. He laved and tasted, suckled and
it
d side her.

ou're wet," he said when his mouth took a break from
k.

Again, she giggled. "Must be the seawater."

"Must be." He crawled over her, covering her body with his, and pressing her deeply into the damp sand. He eased his cock inside her and smiled. "You make me laugh, Candra. I don't think I realized how important that is."

"You haven't laughed enough in your life. You had to remember how."

He kissed her, softly and sweetly, in counterpoint to the gentle rhythm of his thrusts. "And I had to remember what it meant to make love," he said. "And you helped me remember that, too."

And then he did just that. He made love to her, slowly and sweetly, his touch so tender it made her want to weep. And she believed at last that he was happy and complete, and that she had something to do with that.

And perhaps, in his completeness, she had found her own.

Why an electronic book?

We live in the Information Age—an exciting time in the history of human civilization, in which technology rules supreme and continues to progress in leaps and bounds every minute of every day. For a multitude of reasons, more and more avid literary fans are opting to purchase e-books instead of paper books. The question from those not yet initiated into the world of electronic reading is simply: *Why?*

1. *Price.* An electronic title at Ellora's Cave Publishing and Cerridwen Press runs anywhere from 40% to 75% less than the cover price of the exact same title in paperback format. Why? Basic mathematics and cost. It is less expensive to publish an e-book (no paper and printing, no warehousing and shipping) than it is to publish a paperback, so the savings are passed along to the consumer.

2. *Space.* Running out of room in your house for your books? That is one worry you will never have with electronic books. For a low one-time cost, you can purchase a handheld device specifically designed for e-reading. Many e-readers have large, convenient screens for viewing. Better yet, hundreds of titles can be stored within your new library—on a single microchip. There are a variety of e-readers from different manufacturers. You can also read e-books on your PC or laptop computer. (Please note that Ellora's

Cave does not endorse any specific brands. You can check our websites at www.ellorascave.com or www.cerridwenpress.com for information we make available to new consumers.)

3. *Mobility*. Because your new e-library consists of only a microchip within a small, easily transportable e-reader, your entire cache of books can be taken with you wherever you go.

4. ***Personal Viewing Preferences.*** Are the words you are currently reading too small? Too large? Too… ANNOYING? Paperback books cannot be modified according to personal preferences, but e-books can.

5. ***Instant Gratification.*** Is it the middle of the night and all the bookstores near you are closed? Are you tired of waiting days, sometimes weeks, for bookstores to ship the novels you bought? Ellora's Cave Publishing sells instantaneous downloads twenty-four hours a day, seven days a week, every day of the year. Our webstore is never closed. Our e-book delivery system is 100% automated, meaning your order is filled as soon as you pay for it.

Those are a few of the top reasons why electronic books are replacing paperbacks for many avid readers.

As always, Ellora's Cave and Cerridwen Press welcome your questions and comments. We invite you to email us at Comments@ellorascave.com or write to us directly at Ellora's Cave Publishing Inc., 1056 Home Avenue, Akron, OH 44310-3502.

erridwen, the Celtic Goddess of wisdom, was the muse who brought inspiration to story-tellers and those in the creative arts. Cerridwen Press encompasses the best and most innovative stories in all genres of today's fiction. Visit our site and discover the newest titles by talented authors who still get inspired - much like the ancient storytellers did, once upon a time.

CERRÍOWEN PRESS

www.cerrídwenpress.com